The Corpse at Windsor Bridge

Jason Vail

The Corpse at Windsor Bridge

THE CORPSE AT WINDSOR BRIDGE

Copyright 2020, by Jason Vail

A Hawk Publishing book.

Cover design and map by Ashley Barber.

ISBN: 9798647688095

Hawk Publishing
Tallahassee, FL 32312

The Corpse at Windsor Bridge

The Corpse at Windsor Bridge

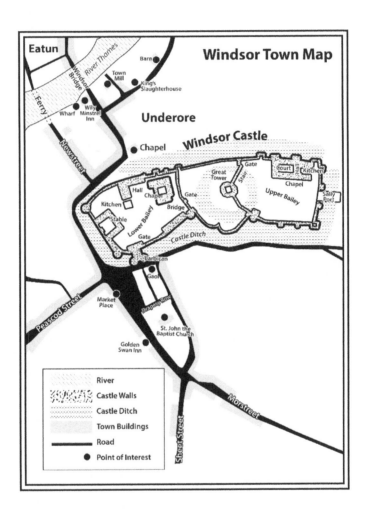

December 1263
to
January 1264

The Corpse at Windsor Bridge

Chapter 1

Stephen Attebrook heard the shouts about a dead man as he neared the northern entrance to the bridge over the River Thames leading to Windsor and its famous castle on the high ridge above the water.

"It's just ahead of you!" shouted one of the bridge toll-takers, who had also been alerted by the calls from the river. He climbed on the railing and was waving to someone in a boat beneath him.

Stephen edged his mare to the railing. Dead men in rivers were not things you happened across every day. When he was a coroner, this would have been a matter of professional concern. But he had put aside that life for a better and more pleasant one. Or so he kept telling himself. Despite a sense of reluctance tinged with revulsion, however, the worm of curiosity niggled. Just a look, he said to himself. I'll take just one small look to see what's what. Then I'll ride on and not think about the sad matter again.

The wooden bridge arched upward to its apex at the middle of the river, and as Stephen reached the top, his perch on horseback enabled a view over the railing, where upriver a flat-bottomed boat was putting away from the southern bank. A boy stood in the bow of the boat, pointing toward the water ahead of him, while a man rowed following his direction.

"I see him!" the boy exclaimed. "He's there! I told you! It's not just some rubbish!"

"Damn it, boy!" the rower shouted back. "I never said it was rubbish! That was your mother!"

Stephen spotted the object in question, a pale dome lapped by wavelets with a crow perched upon it that took wing as the boat came near.

The boy grasped a handful of dark collar and lifted the object, clearly now a body, the head tonsured, as far out of the water as the shoulders before the effort became too much for him, and the corpse sank back into the river.

Stephen had seen drowned people before floating in rivers and there was something odd about this one. Normally, they floated with their limbs outstretched. But the arms of this corpse had been pinned to its sides, nor were the legs visible. But it was not his business, so he thrust such thoughts from his mind, as Gilbert Wistwode clumped up on his mule.

"Dear God, I've never been so happy to see anything in my life!" gasped Gilbert, referring to the castle and not the body, as he had neither heard nor seen what was transpiring below.

For his part, Stephen did not draw Gilbert's attention to the tragedy of a drowned man. One more dead man who was not their concern did not warrant interfering with Gilbert's peace of mind any more than his own.

Gilbert, meanwhile, raised his sore bottom from the saddle of his trusty mule and gave it a rub. They had been riding for a good part of the day over bad, meandering roads taken to avoid lands held by the King's enemies in the midlands.

"Our work is done at last!" Gilbert sighed.

"Not quite," Stephen said.

"What's going on over there?" Gilbert asked, peering in the direction of the rowboat.

"Nothing."

Stephen turned back to get a look at the herd of cattle that he had driven all the way across England from Ludlow for Lord Geoffrey Geneville to deliver to the King's army. The two-hundred-forty-three head (this morning's count) were stamping and huffing in the street of the village of Eatun behind him. The eight drovers and their dogs were having trouble keeping the herd together as the toll-takers dithered over Lord Geoffrey's letter, which was supposed to free them from having to pay tolls, since Stephen was on the king's business. One cow poked a head into the doorway of a shop, eliciting bellows of outrage from someone within it.

"Best get them across before they go on a rampage and tear down the village," Stephen said to Gilbert.

"Are we clear to cross?" Stephen then called to the toll-taker who turned from the spectacle of the dead man to the more mundane business for which he was employed.

"Your letter is in order." The toll-taker held out Stephen's letter of safe conduct.

Stephen waved at the drovers, paused at the north side of the bridge, and squeezed the mare to urge her forward. As the mare ambled down toward the south bank, he glanced up at the castle. It was one of the largest castles in England and reminded him of another in Wales, Cheapstowe, white, solemn and imposing. He chuckled at the name Cheapstowe. In the west country tongue that meant "marketplace," an odd name for a castle.

The drovers got the herd moving, their hoofs thundering on the planks of the bridge, which shook so that for a moment, Stephen felt almost certain it would burst apart and spill the herd into the river.

Above the racket the herd made came the shouts of the drovers, the snap of their whips, and the barks of their dogs, which kept the herd shuffling onward and the odd cow from straying.

Luckily, though, the bridge held firm and the herd made it across that one and a shorter one a bit further on spanning a millrace. The drover leading the procession passed by Stephen and Gilbert who managed to find a safe place to the side, the bell about the lead cow's neck clanking at every swaying step. The drover needed no instruction where to go. He had done this before. The herd flowed around a sharp corner, where the road climbed to the top of the hill toward the castle gates and the paddock to receive the cattle.

Stephen waited until the last of the herd had rounded the bend and the twenty mounted sergeants who brought up the rear crossed the bridge. He had been charged not only with delivering the cattle, but also these men, who had been sent to fulfill knight service for masters who preferred to remain at home. He counted to make sure they were all there, glad that he had not lost any of them — a thing he could not say for the cattle — and then started up the hill himself.

The road turned right to ascend the hill and then bore left around the western walls of the castle. A party of horsemen was coming the other way, but they had paused against some shops, since the herd, as it usually did, had expanded to fill the width of the street, even spilling into the castle ditch so that one cow tumbled and fell to the bottom, dogs racing to bark at the cow's heels as it lumbered up to join its fellows.

The riders were all elegantly dressed, but one stood out from the others. Stephen recognized him as Prince Edward. Edward was a tall man on a grey stallion of at least sixteen hands. He wore a floppy purple hat embroidered with gold that set off the dark blond hair curling to his shoulders. His grey eyes, the left eyelid sagging slightly, regarded the herd with disinterest. The expressions of some of those about him were impatient, however. Edward's lips pursed as if caught up by some thought, and he rubbed his jutting cleft chin with a purple-gloved hand.

Stephen ordered the men to the edge of the castle ditch out of the way of the prince's party as the herd finally jostled up the hill and around the corner to the town market, which lay outside the western gate of the castle.

The prince started down, the others following, one of them with a pair of hawks on his arm.

Ordinarily, princes did not take notice of common people in the street, but the prince reined up and surveyed Stephen and the mounted sergeants. His eyes returned to Stephen.

"I know you," Edward said. "Attebrook, isn't it? From Ludlow."

"It is, your grace," Stephen said. "I am surprised you remember."

Edward's fingers tapped a thigh. "Come looking for a fight, have you?"

"I suppose I have, sir."

Edward smiled slightly. "We'll give you one before long, I think. If you're up to it." He made a vague wave with one hand, a reference to Stephen's injury. Stephen had lost half his left foot in Spain, and those who knew of the infirmity, which seemed to be everyone in England, thought he could not ride a horse well enough to fight.

"I don't think I will have a problem, sir," Stephen said.

Edward urged his horse forward. "Glad to have you, Attebrook. We can use every man! Even if you have trouble staying in the saddle!" he added over his shoulder without looking back.

Stephen broke away from the tail end of the herd and led the sergeants into the castle's lower bailey. He had been told to deliver the men to a Drew de Barentin.

The gate warden inspected the letter Geneville had given him and announced that said Sir Drew had his quarters in the tower on top of the great motte, although he had no idea if Sir Drew was there now; most likely not, since he was the constable and had many duties.

"You'll know him by his white hair and great age," the gate warden said. "He must be eighty," he added, shaking his head that a man could live so long. "Still got all his teeth, too." The warden, satisfied that the pass was genuine and that Stephen and the men presented no threat, waved them through the gate. "You can wait inside just there. Venture no further."

"Thanks," Stephen said.

He eased himself down from the saddle once they were inside the castle, but not without provoking a painful twinge from his right ankle, which he had badly sprained over a month ago. While he could walk without the aid of crutches now, it still hurt.

"Keep an eye on the men," he said to Gilbert. Stephen glanced through the gate to the marketplace, where coming in he had spotted at least three taverns and two inns. He didn't want them making a break for the taverns and getting drunk. If they caused trouble before the handover, he would be the one responsible for any damage they caused. "Don't let any of them out of the castle."

"As if they'll pay attention to what I say," Gilbert muttered. He was a small round man with a small round head fringed with disorderly brown hair. A most unsoldierly looking fellow, the men had teased him about his lack of height and often likened him to a pudding or an ale barrel since they had departed from Ludlow.

"You're the man with the money," Stephen said. "Threaten to dock their pay." Gilbert was along on his venture as the company clerk. He had the men's wages, the last allotment to be paid out when they were handed over to Sir Drew, and was charged with keeping accounts for Geoffrey Geneville, who wanted to be sure his money was properly spent on the men and on the fodder that had been ordered for the herd on the way.

"You tell them," Gilbert said. "You're better at making threats than I am, ones they'll believe anyway."

Stephen did not reply other than with a wave as he limped across the bailey to the other side of the castle, where what looked like a hall stood by the walled grounds of a church. If Sir Drew was anywhere in the lower bailey — a likely prospect since the king and prince were in residence in the upper bailey — it was likely to be in the hall. An old man like him had to be by the fire keeping his ancient bones warm, even if he was supposed to be a busy constable.

Gilbert thrust his cold fingers under his cloak, which he pulled tighter around his shoulders, and stamped feet tingling with the chill. He regretted agreeing to come on this venture for the hundredth time even though he was being well paid for it; God knew, he and his wife needed the money with their inn doing poorly this season. And he liked getting out of the house and away from chores, but it was never long before he wished for the comforts of home, especially the products of his kitchen. The food on the road was always terrible and the fare at inns and taverns along the way was only slightly less so. Sleeping on the cold ground was never much of a treat either.

Mindful of the need to keep an eye on the men, Gilbert counted them to make sure none had slipped away. Fortunately, they all were standing around or sitting on the ground to await developments, and none yet had made a break for the gate. Gilbert was relieved. He was not sure what he would do if any of them tried it. Grasp the malefactor about the leg and plead for him not to go, perhaps?

One of the horses raised her tail, the sign of imminent defecation, which the man sitting on the ground beneath her rump failed to see, although a couple of the other men noticed it. But they said nothing, so that the manure cascaded down on the sitting man's shoulders. He scrambled away to the raucous laughter of the others.

The laughter died, however, when a red-haired, freckled knight pounded through the gate and reined up in front of Gilbert, sending him staggering backward to avoid a collision.

Gilbert recognized the knight as one of those in Prince Edward's entourage, who had passed them on the street, and he was nerving himself up to speak when the knight spat, "Where's Attebrook?"

Gilbert directed a wavering finger at the hall across the bailey. "The hall. He's gone—"

He had no chance to say more, for the knight whipped the horse's head away and dug spurs into his sides. The horse leapt forward and galloped toward the hall, where the knight dismounted before the horse had even stopped. He ran through a small gate in the wall by the church, not the place Gilbert had indicated nor where he had seen Stephen disappear. Gilbert hoped the knight would not come back soon. He would be angry that he had been misdirected.

"You all right?" one of the sergeants asked Gilbert.

"I think so," Gilbert said. At least his voice didn't waver like his finger had done.

"What's that about, do you suppose?"

"I have no idea," Gilbert said. "But it can't be good."

The building Stephen thought was the hall was no such thing. It held chambers for visitors. The hall proper was within the walls surrounding the church. Sir Drew was not in the actual hall, or at least there was no one there matching his description.

Stephen asked a servant bringing in an armful of firewood if he had seen the man, but he hadn't. He asked a few others, who had not laid eyes on the constable all day, and the best guess was that he was in the upper bailey or perhaps out at the army encampment on the flat ground to the east of the castle. Which meant he could be anywhere. Stephen's ankle ached badly and he hated the possibility of having to tramp all over in search of Sir Drew.

He was headed toward the door when it flew open and a tall, resplendently dressed man some years younger than Stephen, who could only be a rich knight or nobleman, strode in, clearly in a hurry.

The man's gaze fastened on Stephen as they took in his appearance. Beneath Stephen's soiled brown traveling cloak could be seen a faded blue woolen coat, a yellow tunic that once had been bright but age and wear had diminished its hue to the color of piss (in Harry the carver's discerning opinion), patched and mended green stockings, and battered old boots in need of replacement. The man frowned in obvious judgment as he pegged Stephen's place on the ladder of society many rungs lower than his and not at all deserving of his meager title of "sir," even if Edward had uttered it without hesitation.

"Attebrook!" the man barked. "I am Gilbert de Clare, earl of Gloucester. Prince Edward requires your attendance!"

"But I just saw him, sir," Stephen said, trying not to sound alarmed at the fact the prince wanted to see him and that he had sent a Marcher earl, one of the most powerful men in the country, to fetch him. "On the road. He was on his way down to the river."

"Don't stand there moving your mouth, man! We must hurry!"

Chapter 2

De Clare didn't wait for Stephen's response. He spun about and rushed out of the hall on long muscular legs.

There was nothing Stephen could do but try to keep up with him.

De Clare had already left the walled enclosure by the time Stephen hobbled to the gate, and was mounting a stallion.

"What's the matter with you?" de Clare demanded as he swung the stallion toward the castle gate.

"Sprained my ankle," Stephen said through gritted teeth.

"Don't let that slow you down," de Clare said. "The prince doesn't like excuses." He trotted his horse toward the castle gate again without awaiting a reply.

Despite his impatience, de Clare waited at the gate for Stephen to catch up and mount his mare.

"What's happening?" Gilbert asked.

"I don't know, but I have a suspicion," Stephen said. "You best come with me."

"Oh, dear," Gilbert stuttered, struggling to mount the mule, who had found a tuft of grass in an otherwise grassless bailey and who defied Gilbert's efforts to drag him away from it.

Stephen looked the men over. They had all come to their feet, aware that something out of the ordinary was transpiring.

"Martin!" he called to the one generally taken to be the group's leader. "No man is to leave this spot until you've seen Sir Drew and been entered into the muster rolls! Have someone find him right away."

"What about our wages?" Martin asked, glancing at Gilbert's satchel, which contained all their money.

"We'll be back to pay you off," Stephen said.

De Clare went through the gate at a trot, picked up a canter on the bridge, pelted through the barbican, and turned right, passing out of view.

Stephen urged the mare into a canter after him; the gate wardens at the main gate dodged against the stone walls.

Those within the barbican, warned by this, ducked into doorways on either side of the passage.

"Wait!" Gilbert cried, still struggling with the mule; he had one foot momentarily in a stirrup, but the mule shied away and he fell heavily.

"You'll find us at the bridge!" Stephen called over his shoulder as the mare thundered over the bridge and he turned right after de Clare who had already disappeared around the far tower of the castle.

Stephen caught up with de Clare on the sloping road beneath the north wall of the castle shortly before the street turned toward the bridge.

"How do you know we're going to the bridge?" de Clare snarled as they pounded around the corner.

"I saw a dead man being pulled from the river there when we crossed," Stephen said. "Although I don't know what interest the prince could have in such a thing."

"Ordinarily, he wouldn't." De Clare did not say anything more. His blue eyes were grim, thin lips pressed together.

Eight horses stood riderless at the southern end of the bridge, held by a pair of squires.

De Clare reined up by them and leaped off his horse. He clambered down the steep bank to the footpath just above the water, where the prince was kneeling by the dead man with the others of his party clustered about him, handkerchiefs over their mouths against a choking, familiar stench that made Stephen's guts curl even from the street. The man and boy in the rowboat who had recovered the body were nearby, hats over their mouths, looking frightened.

Edward stood up as de Clare reached him. His eyes went over de Clare's shoulders to Stephen.

Stephen limped slowly down the bank. It was rough going on his two bad feet, even though the descent was made easier for the ordinary person by the path that led downward from the street. He didn't want to fall and embarrass himself any more than his mere presence would.

The Corpse at Windsor Bridge

"You sent for me, your grace?" Stephen asked as he halted before the prince.

Edward nodded, but did not speak. There were tear tracks on his face and droplets caught on the tips of his day-old beard. He motioned behind him. The entourage stepped away so Stephen could see the body.

"A friend," Stephen said.

"Yes," Edward said.

It was hard to see how anyone could recognize the man, which was not unusual for bodies that had been in the water for some time; Stephen had seen his share of them the past year. The dead man's face was grotesquely swollen, a caricature of humanity, a gargoyle that had leaped off a church's frieze to become rotting flesh: the eyes clamped shut, the cheeks impossibly puffy, the mouth round with protruding lips and tongue sticking out as if mocking those who dared to watch; the visible flesh sloughing off in places and bluish and mottled yellow at others in nauseating profusion. The body as well had swelled, pressing outward against a priest's brown habit so that the fabric barely constrained the corruption, giving it the appearance of a fat belly lapping over a waist belt that the man had never displayed in life, likely to burst at the slightest touch.

The man's arms were tied to his belt on either side of the buckle with lengths of leather rope.

The legs projecting from the skirt of the habit were equally swollen and bluish yellow, though down at the ankles they were a bright red.

The feet were bound at the ankles with leather rope as well, one end dangling away.

Stephen knelt by that rope. The dangling end had been cut with a knife.

"He did not just fall in the river," Stephen said.

"No," Edward said. "I believe he had some help." He waved at the boatman and the boy. "Tell him what you found."

The boatman pointed at the rope about the corpse's ankles and said through his hat, "There was a stone tied to his legs, sir."

"You cut it away, why?" Stephen asked.

"We couldn't get him in the boat otherwise."

Stephen rose as Gilbert stumbled down the bank and paused at the bottom, taking in the horrible scene. Intimidated by the assembly and the presence of the prince, Gilbert remained where he was.

"What was his name?" Stephen asked. The thing at his feet, disgusting as it was, had been a person, and at least he should think of him by his name.

"Giles de Twet," Edward said. "I require that you find who killed him."

Stephen was so appalled at this order that his mind froze. The men in the entourage were speaking but the words were fuzzy and sounded as if they were far away. His mind focused on useless details: some way down the town wharf was a shack, little more than a lean-to; a good half dozen raggedly dressed children watched him, Edward and the dead man. Some of the children were laughing and pushing each other; others were grave, one or two had cloths over their noses and mouths against the stench.

Stephen wanted to protest that he had had more than his fill of investigating mysterious deaths. His mouth moved to say something, but he stopped himself before any sound emerged.

"You have some objection?" Edward asked coldly.

"No, your grace," Stephen mumbled. As much as he wanted to refuse, such a direct order from the prince had to be obeyed.

"Good, then," Edward said. He turned to go.

Thoughts of what had to be done ran through Stephen's head, one after the other. He had done this sort of thing often enough now that he merely had to repeat what had become something of a ritual, at least to get started.

"I will need some place to examine Father Giles," Stephen said. "Somewhere that prying eyes are not privy to."

"What for?" Edward asked, half turning back.

Stephen could have used allusions and circumlocutions to make his point, but directness seemed a better course with Edward, who did not have much patience.

"I need to cut off his clothes and examine every inch of him," Stephen said.

"What for?" Edward stammered, appalled at the idea.

"To see what killed him."

"Isn't that obvious?" one of the assembled noblemen cried. "He drowned!"

"No, sir, it is not obvious," Stephen said. "He was found in the river, but that doesn't mean he was alive when he went in."

"I don't see what difference that makes," Gilbert de Clare spat.

"It may mean he was killed elsewhere and then brought to the river," Stephen said. "In that case there may be witnesses."

"They would have been found already," de Clare said. "We turned the town upside down for more than a week after Giles disappeared."

"I still need to examine him," Stephen said.

"It is a desecration," another of the nobles said. "Get him buried, and fast." He waved a hand before his nose, which he scrunched up.

"Yes, he needs burial, but not until I'm done," Stephen said.

He turned to Edward. What happened now was up to him.

Edward's expression relaxed a bit. He nodded. "I have heard about Sir Stephen's methods. There's a chapel up the street. Have Giles taken there."

He started off to the street, leaving Stephen by the body with a mind bubbling with questions. Stephen hurried after him and caught up at the steps.

"My lord," Stephen said, restraining himself from laying a hand on Edward's sleeve to keep him from getting away. "A final word."

Edward turned abruptly. "What?"

"You said a search had been conducted for de Twet. Who was in charge of it?"

"Why?"

"Knowing what has already been done will save time and needless duplication of effort."

"Of course. Adam Rykelyng is his name." As if Edward thought that was enough, his other foot went up two steps.

"Where can he be found, my lord?" Stephen asked. "Is he among those men?" He indicated the others now right behind him at the foot of the stairs.

"No," Edward said. "His quarters are in the lower bailey. Is that all?"

It was clear Edward was losing patience with Stephen's questions, so Stephen said, "Yes, my lord. It is."

"Good. I am leaving for France with the king one week from today. I would like this matter cleared up by then."

"I'll do my best, but I can't promise results in so short a time."

"Why is it that when I ask for even a simple thing to be done all I hear from people is excuses?"

Edward and the entourage climbed the stepped path to the street. They mounted their horses and rode back to the castle after the squires were ordered to find porters for the body and something to carry it on. The squires simply grabbed those nearby, a few shopkeepers and a couple of men walking over the bridge. Those who protested when they discovered why they were needed had their minds changed by being lashed with riding whips and through assorted kicks and punches.

Father Giles had been a tall man in life and, allowing for the distortion done to his corpse by rot, a well-set up one, too, in the same leanly muscular way as Stephen himself. Gazing at the body, Stephen thought morosely that if he lay down beside it, Gilbert would note they were about the same height.

This made for a rather large corpse, and no single board long and wide enough to serve could be found, and the squires were on the brink of tearing down the door to a glover's shop by the bridge when some boys came forward with three narrow boards from a rear yard. The body was lifted upon these boards, one at the shoulders, the second at the waist and the third at the thighs.

The porters gagged so violently that they tottered to and fro, placing their cargo in danger of pitching to the ground. The squires, mindful of this risk, shouted threats and encouragement to the porters, who were one on each end of a board, and they shuffled toward the rising ground by the bridge.

Negotiating this rise brought further chances of tipping the body to the ground, but somehow, they struggled to the street and headed southward toward the castle.

The chapel in question sat protected by a low stone fence where the street turned right and began its climb up castle hill.

Three black-robed monks inhabited the place, and they peered from the window of their little house by the stone chapel. They had been warned what was coming and watched aghast as the sorry procession crossed the yard and invaded the chapel.

The place was bare inside, except for a wooden altar at the back and behind it on the wall a painted crucifix of Our Lord, his blue robe lined with golden paint and golden fleur de lis on it.

"Put him down over there," Stephen said, pointed to a spot by a window which offered some light.

The porters set the body down and, seeing their opportunity, rushed for the doorway before the squires could require anything more of them.

"Will that be all, sir?" the eldest squire, who had taken charge of the others, asked.

"You can go," Stephen said. "Oh, did your instructions say anything about rounding up gravediggers?"

"No, sir," the squire said.

"You might speak to the monks about that, if you would be so kind."

"Of course, sir."

"Can I go, too?" Gilbert said from the doorway as the squires hurried around him, as anxious to be gone as the townspeople had been.

"You know you can't." Stephen knelt by the body and fumbled for his gloves. They were old calf skin but in good shape, and he hated to ruin them. But he wasn't touching the dead man or his clothing with bare hands. He glanced at Gilbert. "Get a shroud from those monks. We're going to need something to cover him when we're done. And ask if they can spare a table."

Gilbert returned with a linen sheet and reported that the monks were unwilling to surrender a table, since they could guess what it was wanted for.

"They didn't want to give me the sheet, either," Gilbert said, kneeling beside Stephen, his face screwed up in distaste at the stench. "They demanded money."

"What did you say?"

"I told them this was Prince Edward's dear friend, and if they wanted money to do him honor, then they would have to get it from him."

"Well played."

"I have my moments."

"You certainly do. Let this be one more of them. Let's get on with it, then." Stephen knelt by the body.

Gilbert's face tightened even more with distaste and horror. "Look at the time you've wasted while I've been running your errand! You could have had him out of his robe by now!"

"You're going to make a fuss about this, are you?" Stephen demanded indignantly. "It's your turn."

"I examined the last one," Gilbert said archly. "It's *your* turn." The *last one* had been an elderly lady who had fallen down a flight of stairs a week ago, when they had been summoned to look her over even though neither of them held an official position; for some reason people still acted as if Stephen still was a coroner. Perhaps it was because in the political confusion of the dispute between the barons under Simon de Montfort and the king, the replacement who had been appointed was a Montfort man based at Hereford, and Ludlow leaned toward the king's party. That examination had not required the cutting off of her clothes. A glance at the great dent in the old woman's forehead was enough to determine the cause of death.

"This is hardly fair."

Gilbert looked stubborn.

"All right," Stephen relented, mainly because the quicker this business was done, the quicker the both of them could get away from the choking rot. "Be that way. Let's have a look at his hands first."

Stephen bent over those hands, blue as stones. There were two rings on the right hand and one on the left pinkie. Two were silver and one, which held a stone the color of seawater in a harbor on a sunny day, was gold. Instead of being tied directly to the belt, the ropes securing each hand were fastened to the belt with a square knot. There was a short length of rope to the strands about the wrists, three or four inches or so, and knots securing the wrists were slip knots pulled fast so that the rope had sunk deeply into the swollen flesh. On the right wrist just above the rope was a thin gold bracelet. Stephen tried to free the slip knots but could not, so he cut the strands connecting the hands to the man's belt.

Now for the habit. He grasped the dead man's collar and sawed through the fabric in the direction of his feet. He paused to undo the belt, squinting in expectation of an eruption, but none came and he finished, with some struggle.

He lay the wings of the garment aside and looked at the body. The stomach was as taut and distended as a full wine skin, and had burst, the intestines dribbling through a hole in the side. The color of the skin was the same blue-and-yellow as the face. Removal of the man's clothing revealed a delicate golden cross around his neck on a chain that also appeared to be gold, which he had worn underneath his habit.

Stephen drew the chain around the dead man's head. The object rested in his hand, too beautiful to be cast aside without examination. The chain was composed of small links so fragile and fine that they seemed beyond the capacity of a smith to fashion. The cross, the stem of which was no longer than his middle finger supporting a figure of Christ with arms outstretched, was equally delicate. The eyes, nose and mouth were finely rendered, as were the waves of the hair falling to the figure's shoulders and the curls of the beard. The fingers and toes were also carved, so impossibly small, and even the finger- and toenails had been etched in. The figure's feet rested on a ruby that glowed dully red in the bad light of the chapel, but would burn bright in the daylight to dazzle the eye. The thing must have cost a fortune, tens of pounds at least. It was a remarkable thing to find on a dead man, and spoke to the fact that he must have come from a prominent and wealthy family.

He set aside the bauble in the dirt, bent over and, holding his breath against the choking stench, looked closely at the man's face, his lips, his ears, his neck. Then he worked his way down to the feet.

"Nothing, eh?" Gilbert said, hands over his mouth and nose, not that did any good.

Stephen shook his head.

"No sign of smothering?" Gilbert asked, hovering a few steps away, his mouth muffled by the hem of his shirt. They had learned that someone who had been smothered often displayed little scarlet marks, like pinpricks, about the face and eyes.

"Not that I can see."

"And no marks on the neck. So, he wasn't strangled."

"No. I don't see any bruises or wounds. Let's get him turned over."

Gilbert hung back, and could not be coaxed to come forward with the dark looks Stephen shot in his direction. Stephen tugged and twisted the corpse's shoulders to bring it around on its stomach.

Gilbert still did not help as Stephen wormed Giles' arms out of his sleeves and removed the habit, which he tossed aside.

Gilbert fished the belt from the pile with the point of his knife and found a fat purse. He weighed it on his palm, bouncing a little so that the coins within it made a faint, musical sound.

"It's pretty heavy," Gilbert said. He glanced at the gold cross lying nearby. "Doesn't look like robbery."

"No," Stephen agreed. "Whoever killed him wasn't interested in theft. He was wearing enough gold."

"And there's this." Gilbert plucked up the belt with two fingers and held it out.

"What am I supposed to see?"

"He had a knife," Gilbert said, indicating the leather scabbard of a small utility knife dangling from the belt, the kind of knife that everyone carried, including most women. "It's not here."

"Do you think it fell out?"

"Do you? They're normally held pretty snugly."

"Yes, they are. Someone accosted him, he pulled the knife and then was overpowered?" Stephen speculated.

Stephen was going over the man's back head to toe when the chapel door opened and three women entered.

Two of the women, who had the look of ladies' maids, recoiled in horror, hands over their mouths, and gasped.

The other woman, a lady by her red silk overgown with slit sides covering a light blue satin gown covered with yellow flowers and white silk wimple, said in continental French without turning to look at them, "You may go. There is no need for you to see this."

"But, my lady," one of the attendants gasped in court French, "to leave you alone here, with two men? We cannot!"

"I suspect I will be safe enough. Leave the door open, if it troubles you."

The two attendants curtseyed and went out, standing just outside, peering in.

The lady stood still, hands at her sides, head high, her face composed as a statue's. Only a slight twitch at the corners of her small mouth betrayed any agitation. She was young, no more than twenty, her skin smooth and pale, appearing more so when matched with her black hair. In the spare light of the chapel, dim and almost grey, she seemed beautiful, although she had a long, narrow face that left her just short of it in actuality. Yet, a striking, attractive woman nonetheless.

She strode across the chapel and stood above Stephen and the body.

"What happened to him?" she asked. "How did he die?"

"I don't know," Stephen said. He knew he should rise, bow, or something, and tried to rise, but his right ankle failed him and he collapsed to his knees. He bowed his head slightly. "You'll have to forgive me, my lady. I have an injury."

The lady ignored his excuse and said instead, "I am told you are an expert on these matters."

"Even experts don't know everything."

The woman's nostrils flared. "I have seen that. Will you be able to tell, eventually?"

"I can't tell you that either, for certain."

"He was murdered, though."

"I would say that is a good guess."

The woman knelt. Stephen sensed a perfume that must have been expensive. She held a hand over the tonsured head as if she meant to touch it. The hand hovered there and then withdrew. "Blood of the devil," she muttered, not in continental French, but in Castilian.

"Poor Giles," she said, reverting to French, and snapped. "Turn him over. I want to see his face."

"That's not wise, my lady," Stephen said in Castilian. "You will not know him. He is … deformed."

The lady's head jerked up. "You understand me?" she asked.

"*Sí*," Stephen said.

"You are not Castilian. Where did you learn to speak like that?"

"On the border with Andalusia."

"An Englishman in Andalusia. You must have been fighting the Moors."

"Yes."

"Well." She paused and drew a breath. "Please turn him over, then. If you would be so kind." Although her tone was no longer harshly commanding and was phrased as a request, there was no mistaking the order in it. And there was about her the air of a woman used to having her commands obeyed.

Stephen did not know who she was, but she clearly was well-connected. He sighed, grasped the shoulders and turned Giles on his back.

As he did so, the lady picked up the gold chain and crucifix. She cupped them in her hands, one over the other and held them close.

He watched the lady for some sign of revulsion at the ugliness of the corpse, but her face was frozen rock hard. Then the mouth trembled.

"A friend of yours?" Stephen asked.

"Yes. He was my confessor and chaplain. I will keep this in remembrance of him." She put the chain and crucifix in her belt pouch, stood and paced away. "I simply can't believe he's dead. Who would want to murder such a gentle soul?"

Silence reigned for a moment.

"Why are you here?" Stephen asked.

The lady's eyes narrowed. She regarded Stephen as if affronted at being asked. Then the eyes relaxed and returned to Giles. "I wanted to know if he suffered in death. Clearly, you cannot tell me."

"Not yet."

"When you know, I want to hear it."

"And whom should I ask for if I have something to say?"

"I am Isabel Gascelyn, lady in waiting and cousin to Princess Leonor. You know of her, of course? Prince Edward's wife?"

Isabel went out of the church into the fading light of an approaching evening.

Gilbert grasped his heart and fell back against a wall when Stephen told him who the lady was.

"You thick-headed lout! You mean, you were arguing with a Spanish lady? Someone close to the princess?" Gilbert gasped. "How could you not know who she was?"

"Did you know?"

"Well, no. But it was clear she is someone at court. Everyone knows you must tip-toe around such people."

"Did it sound like an argument?" Stephen asked.

"Some people might have thought your tone was impertinent, although I have no way of telling about your words once you began conversing in that foreign tongue." Gilbert shook his head. "Whatever — you are ruined at court. Simply ruined. Did you not give the least thought to the fact you might need Edward's favor to get your manor back? And here you've shown disrespect to one of his wife's courtiers! That will surely get back to him! It surely will!"

Stephen stooped for the linen sheet. His older brother William had inherited the family manor, Hafton, upon the death of their father. Then William had died unexpectedly last year. According to law, Stephen should have the manor as William's closest male relative. But William's widow, Elysande, had possession of it claiming by right her daughter, Ida, and the argument that William had adopted her and made her his heir. She was a stubborn, determined woman, and the claims would have to be settled by lawyers, judges and appeals to the crown. Meanwhile, the crown technically held seisin of the manor because Ida, at nearly seventeen, was not yet married and the proper heir was identified and had sworn fealty to the king.

"Did you happen to think to ask for a needle and thread?" Stephen asked.

"Yes," Gilbert said, digging into his belt pouch. "Here. Always prepared, always thinking ahead, unlike some people here."

Stephen accepted the needle and thread and turned back to the corpse. "Why don't you go check on the progress of the gravediggers. I'll shroud him. There's no telling how long it will be for a friend to show up to do it, and the sooner he's buried the better for everyone. We can't leave him to lie here overnight."

Chapter 3

Stephen and Gilbert remained at the chapel until the grave was dug, and Giles lowered into it and covered up. In the ordinary case, the deceased went to his rest surrounded by friends and family, accompanied by an appropriate funeral service with fine words, praises and final prayers. But the body was so corrupt that it seemed a violation to leave it unburied, so it was a hasty and lonely departure. No one else was there but them and the gravediggers. No priest nor monk came from the little chapter house by the chapel to give a prayer or say anything. It was a sad end for anyone, let alone someone who had, in life, been well connected. For he had been that, if Lady Isabel had known him and the prince wanted to find out who killed him.

"I can't stand it," Gilbert said, as the gravediggers filed out of the yard. "This isn't right. Let us pray for him, at least, even if we didn't know him."

He lowered his head, and Stephen did likewise. Gilbert muttered a brief prayer in Latin so low that Stephen could not make out what he said.

He didn't ask to be enlightened. They crossed themselves and left the yard.

It was dark by the time they rode up to the west gate, which had closed for the night.

Stephen hammered on the barbican gate, and one of the wardens opened a little panel at head height to get a look at him. The warden demanded, "Show me your token."

"I don't have a token," Stephen said. "I've been on business for the prince. It kept us late."

"No token, no admittance after dark. Those are the rules, unless you're a messenger."

"I'm not a messenger."

"Then get out of here and quit bothering me."

As Stephen was about to turn away, the inner gate in the main wall and then the barbican gate opened. Ten men came through. One of them gathered the men around him and said,

"Be back here in two hours. If you're not, you'll have to sleep in the ditch."

The group broke up and fanned out across the marketplace to the taverns and inns identifiable in the dark by the lights around the windows and the riotous noise floating across the way that was only partly muffled by the walls.

"I don't fancy sleeping under any more trees," Gilbert grumbled, drawing his cloak close about him against the descending chill. "And we've missed supper."

"You never forget about your stomach, do you," Stephen said.

"It is the most substantial part of me, after all," Gilbert said, patting his belly with some pride. "I hate to see it diminished."

"I don't want to be responsible for harming such a national treasure. We've quite a choice here, it seems." Stephen gestured toward the dozen or so establishments doing business after dark. "Pick one. As long as the food doesn't lead me to vomit and the beds are free of bugs, I'll not complain."

"Very well," Gilbert said, finger on his lips. "That one." He pointed to an inn across Morstreet from a large church some distance away, where four of the soldiers were just going in. Light from the doorway illuminated a sign over the door bearing a golden swan with one webbed foot on top of a small barrel that was tipped over and pouring a stream of liquid into the mouth of a frog. "If they like it, I doubt we'll be poisoned."

"Clever," Stephen said reining the mare around toward the inn. "I hope it's not too expensive."

"Can't we claim this as expenses? We're still on Geneville's business."

"Yes, I suppose we can. We're not likely to see any reward from the prince when this is done. He probably expects us to work out of love for the crown."

"Let's just hope it doesn't take too long. A week of knocking our heads against a stone wall and then declaring the mystery unsolvable should do it, don't you think?"

Stephen slumped in the saddle. "Maybe."

"It should. After all, the man went missing a week or more ago. They made an inquiry and learned nothing. How could the prince realistically expect more out of us?"

"If he was a rational man, he wouldn't. But I've a feeling he isn't rational about this. We'll just have to see."

Stephen put up the horses in the stable behind the inn and went inside. Gilbert already had a table in a cold corner, a small thing shielded from the fire by the bodies occupying the other tables.

Stephen squeezed his six-foot frame into the small space between wall and table. He was taller than most men and was always having to curl up like this, or bumping his head on door frames and ceiling beams.

He removed his knit cap, which he tucked into his belt, and ran his hands through his long black hair to keep it from falling into his face, thinking it was in need of a trim. Barbers could be expensive, though. Maybe better to wait until they got back to Ludlow, where Joan, his housekeeper, would do it for free. He didn't like to pinch pennies, but he was getting low on ready cash. He once had quite a bit of money, but he had given Gilbert and his wife a large portion of it for a quarter interest in their Ludlow inn, the Broken Shield, so they could pay off a loan. The inn, however, was not doing well owing to the winter and the coming war between supporters of the king and the barons rallying around Simon de Montfort, which curtailed travel. It would be a long time before he saw any return.

Gilbert broke the loaf in half, and drank from his mug. "Not bad. Tastes fresh."

"Is there any meat or cheese? And what about butter?"

"That's coming."

While he waited, Stephen's gaze wandered to those crowding the inn. It was doing brisk business for a Friday evening, and there was hardly a spare seat at any of the tables. Servants hurried to and fro with mugs of ale and food, squeezing through gaps between the bodies and fending off efforts to snatch refreshment not meant for them. In the far corner, Stephen caught a glimpse of the earl who had summoned him from the castle, Gilbert de Clare, with his head against that of a handsome blonde woman who was intent on what Gilbert was saying, nodding now and then, smiling, and occasionally making a brief comment. The blonde girl, who was dressed as a well-off merchant's wife might be, put a hand on the earl's arm, a gesture of shocking familiarity. Yet de Clare did not seem offended. He looked glum at something the woman said and nodded agreement.

Not far away, Stephen spotted another of the young nobles who had been in Edward's escort earlier. He had a pretty girl on his lap. The young fellow removed the girl's yellow scarf and tossed it away. They then kissed passionately and the young man ran a hand up her skirt. She opened her legs for the wandering hand.

An inn often had its own stable of whores, but this establishment seemed to have more than what it should ordinarily support. There were at least seven of them, all dressed better than the average whore, and distinguished from the local women about the tables by their yellow scarves. In addition to being better dressed, they were all young and good-looking, some of them actually pretty, and they circulated about the throng of men, laughing and joking with them. Now and then, one of the whores would depart for the upper chambers with men in hand, while others came down and started their game of flirtation and selection again.

One of them, a small thing with bright red hair, reached Stephen's table and settled on his lap. She put her arms around his neck, and said, "I'm Jennet, handsome, and you are?"

"Stephen Attebrook."

"Just come in? I haven't seen you before."

Stephen nodded. "This afternoon."

"And whose party are you with, not that it's my business?"

"My own."

"Oh! You have your own men? I'll say, I've seen leading men better dressed. You can't have brought many with you, now, can you."

It seemed like pointless banter, but there was something about the questions that made Stephen think she was really interested in the answers. Why she would be, he was not sure.

"Just my friend here," Stephen said, nodding toward Gilbert.

"He doesn't look like much of a soldier," Jennet said, pouting her lips.

"I'm not," Gilbert volunteered as a servant delivered trenchers of sliced pork, cabbage soup and a bowl of butter. "I'm an innkeeper."

"An innkeeper? Looking to snoop out Johnnie's trade secrets, are you?" Jennet laughed. It was a hollow laugh, though, as if she was disappointed with what she had heard.

"Johnnie?" Gilbert asked, dipping a chunk of bread into the cabbage soup.

"That's him, over there," she said, indicating a tall, well-built man with wide shoulders and a brown beard by the taps. "It's his inn you're in."

She ruffled Stephen's hair. "Finish your supper, my pretty lad. I will be back for you."

It was odd to be addressed as a "pretty lad" by a girl who couldn't be more than sixteen or seventeen, and Stephen was twenty-seven.

Jennet eased herself out of Stephen's lap, took a few steps and settled onto another man's lap, and began asking him similar questions.

"That seemed a bit off," Gilbert said.

"It did," Stephen replied. He smoothed his hair and tried a slice of pork which was tender and delicious, not the boot leather he had expected.

"You think she'll be back?"

"I have a feeling she will not."

"Not handsome enough after all, then?"

"You know looks have nothing to do with it."

"Of course, not. You could look like a dead chicken, which you often do in the mornings. Did she lift your purse?"

"No, it's still here."

"Well, then, a real mystery for a change." Gilbert tucked into his supper in earnest, not really interested in solving it.

"I suppose it is."

Across the hall, a mud-spattered man dressed in black with the thigh-high boots of a professional courier climbed the stairs behind one of the pretty whores, who made a show of wagging her ample behind in his face.

De Clare spoke into the blonde woman's ear. She giggled. He rose and extended a hand to her.

The woman smiled up at him, and said something Stephen could not hear over the hubbub. De Clare chuckled. The woman drew on a blue woolen cloak with silver stitching on the hem and accepted de Clare's hand, and the two ventured up the stairs as well.

Chapter 4

Stephen and Gilbert presented themselves at the castle barbican early following morning and stated their business to the sergeant in charge of the watch, who leaned on his spear and eyed them with suspicion.

"I need to speak to Sir Adam Rykelyng," Stephen said.

"Do you have a pass?"

Stephen handed over Geneville's letter.

"This says that you're delivering mounted sergeants for the army," the warden said. "I don't see no mounted sergeants."

"I delivered them yesterday."

"Then your business here is done. Be away."

"Prince Edward asked me to inquire into the death of one Giles de Twet. I'm sure you've heard of him."

"Who, the Prince? Everybody's heard of him."

"I was speaking of de Twet."

"Oh."

"So, did you know Father Giles?" Stephen asked.

"I may have seen him a time or two."

"When did you see him?"

"He went out on occasion."

"When?"

"In the evenings. I saw him a few times when I was going off watch," the gate warden said.

"Where did he go?"

"I couldn't say. Didn't pay no attention."

"Who might know?"

"Robbie might be able to tell you."

"Who's Robbie?"

"He's sergeant-in-charge of the gate on the first night watch," the warden said.

"Where is he now?" Stephen asked.

"Asleep, most likely at this hour."

"Does he have quarters in the gate?" Unmarried wardens usually slept in one of the towers on either side of the gate.

"Nah, he lives in the village," the warden said.

"Where, exactly?"

"You going to bother him now?"

"I'll wait till noon. He should be up by then, shouldn't he?" Stephen asked.

"It's the last house on the right in Morstreet," the warden said.

"Where's that?" Stephen asked.

"Go past the churchyard to the fork. Take the left. It's the road to Stanes."

"Now, about Sir Adam," Stephen said.

"What about him?"

"I must see him."

"I expect he's busy now. All the prince's court are preparing for Father Giles' funeral Mass."

"When will that be?"

"At the third hour."

"I suppose we could just go down and wait until he shows up," Stephen said to Gilbert, who was admiring the stones of the tower.

"Go down? Where might that be?" the warden asked.

"At that little chapel on the way to the river."

"Oh, the Mass isn't to be said at Saint Mary's. They're having it at Saint George's Chapel." The warden hooked a thumb behind him to the church in the lower bailey a short distance away. "Because of the smell. I hear the body fouled the air of Saint Mary's. Can't have folks gagging and choking and catching some terrible disease during such a solemn occasion. And I heard the king was going to be present. He don't like dank smells, and we can't make the king unhappy, can we? Easier to do it here, you know. Less fuss."

It was clear that the warden was not going to budge about letting them in, so Stephen said, "I would like to see the officer of the watch."

"Ah, you would, would you?" The brow of one eye dropped as if he had something in it. There was nothing like asking to see a man's superior officer to ingratiate yourself.

"Yes. Now. Before the sun goes down."

"All right, all right." The warden turned to one of his fellows standing in a tower door. "Bill, fetch Sir Roderick. This gentleman wants a word with him."

Bill disappeared and footsteps could be heard as he ascended the stairwell.

The sound of footsteps resumed after quite a time, then a short, broad and balding man emerged from the doorway.

"What is it, Harry?" the knight asked. He seemed a bit irritated at being summoned.

"My lord," the warden said, "this man wants a word with you."

Sir Roderick's grey eyes wandered over Stephen and Gilbert.

"I remember you," Roderick said.

Stephen nodded. "We arrived yesterday, to deliver men for service in the army."

"Right, with a herd of cattle too, wasn't it?"

"The prince has engaged us to look into the death of Father Giles," Stephen said. "Perhaps you've heard about it."

"I did, in fact. Don't know why it's necessary. We scoured the town only two weeks ago. I doubt we left much for you to uncover."

"That may well be. But I am obliged to try, like it or not. I need access to the castle to do this. Your man here insists that I need a pass."

Roderick sighed. "He's just doing his job. We can't be too careful around here. There's a great fear of spies, and there's talk of a move to assassinate the king and the prince. Can't allow just any old Tom or Dick in. You understand."

"Fully. So, we will need a pass. For the both of us."

"That won't be necessary. I'll inform the watch that you're permitted to enter."

"Day and night."

"Certainly."

Stephen paused before replying, thinking about something Roderick had just said. "So, Father Giles disappeared two weeks ago?"

"Walked right out this gate on a Saturday evening just as we were closing up."

"Did you see where he went?"

"The last look any of my boys had of him, he was walking across the marketplace."

One of the servants Stephen snagged in the hall rapped on the door of the chamber in the chamber block.

"What is it?" a man's voice called impatiently from within.

"A visitor, my lord," the servant replied.

"What's his name?"

The servant looked inquiringly at Stephen.

"Stephen Attebrook," Stephen said. "And Gilbert Wistwode."

"That's Sir Stephen," Gilbert said.

"Of course," the servant said. "Sir Stephen Attebrook and his man, Master Wistwode!"

"A moment!" the voice called back.

"I'll leave you to it, sir," the servant said. He hurried away.

Stephen and Gilbert waited in the hallway. Around them were thumpings, murmurings, voices calling out for this and that article of clothing, valets rushing in and out of chambers on this floor; in short, a hubbub of activity.

"Do you think they're all getting ready for the mass?" Gilbert asked. "It seems a bit much for a lady-in-waiting's chaplain."

"There must be more to the man than we know," Stephen said.

The door opened. A man about Stephen's age stood before them. He was tall, but not as tall as Stephen. His black hair was cut unfashionably short and his beard was also trimmed close and came to a square below his chin. He was dressed in yellow and green stockings but no shoes or boots, a linen shirt so white and fresh that the sun glinting off it would blind the eye, all fashionable and new. The man's dark eyes wandered up and down Stephen from his battered, travel-worn boots, stained and patched stockings and muddy coat.

"Sir Stephen Attebrook, are you?" the fellow said.

"I assume you're Adam Rykelyng," Stephen said.

"In the flesh, unfortunately." Rykelyng frowned and half turned. "Oh, you might as well come on in. When I heard about you, I knew you'd show up at my doorstep eventually. We might as well get this over with. You've caught me in the middle of dressing for Mass."

"Sorry," Stephen said as he entered with Gilbert behind him.

Rykelyng plopped on a bench and began pulling on new, well tooled shoes made of flimsy leather that bore more of a resemblance to a slipper than a shoe. "You'll have to excuse me while I finish. What do you want to know?"

He felt around behind him for a flagon and two cups. He gave Stephen one of the cups, poured wine in both of them. "Sorry there's nowhere else to sit. You can use the bed, if you want."

Stephen settled on the bed while Gilbert remained standing by the door.

"I'm told that you were in charge of the search for Father Giles," Stephen asked.

Rykelyng made a face. "Yes. Damned sorry duty that turned out to be."

"What is your connection with Prince Edward?"

"I'm a household knight."

"Ah, of course."

"I'm told you're a knight yourself. You hardly look like one."

"Knighted in Spain. I don't have any property, though." When people of the gentle class said property, they meant land. Stephen had none, although he had a chest with gold and silver buried beneath the floor of his hall; a rapidly depleting chest that would be empty before long.

The Corpse at Windsor Bridge

Rykelyng chuckled without humor. "I know how that is. I just came into an estate myself — married a little heiress who came available."

"Tell me what you know about Father Giles' disappearance."

Rykelyng drank from the cup and rested it on a knee. "All I know is that he walked out the main gate on a Saturday evening two weeks ago and was last seen crossing from the barbican into Morstreet. Two days after the Feast of Saint Nicholas, it was."

"No one saw him enter any of the inns or taverns? There's quite a lot of them on Morstreet."

"Yes, it's practically wall-to-wall sin and perdition there. Well, my first thought was he went to the Golden Swan. Giles had been going there quite a lot recently. Drowning some sorrow, or something. He wore a sad look those last few weeks. But, he didn't, as far as I found out."

"What did you do to find out?"

"I went round to the Swan myself and asked the proprietor. He said he hadn't seen Giles that night. So, I sent men to ask at every house and place of business in town. Not a sign of him."

"Could he have left town?"

"I doubt it. None of his property was gone. His valet said he left behind in his chamber money and jewels enough to buy two manors. Every parcel of clothing was where he left it, and his valet insisted that nothing was missing, except for the stuff that was out for washing, and that consisted of his traveling clothes. His horses were in the stable. A fine coarser he is, too. Worth a pretty penny. Giles was not the sort of man to go anywhere on foot if he could ride."

"Why were Father Giles' traveling clothes at the laundry, sir?" Gilbert asked.

Rykelyng regarded Gilbert with narrowed eyes as if surprised that he was in the room.

"My assistant," Stephen said. "He often thinks of things I don't."

"Because they were dirty, I suppose?" Rykelyng said shortly.

"Had he gone anywhere recently?" Gilbert persisted.

"I didn't ask," Rykelyng said, his answer even more short than the previous one.

"No matter," Stephen murmured to steer the questioning away from this subject. Rykelyng clearly didn't like being asked about it, especially by Gilbert. "Where can we find this valet?"

"His quarters are in the upper bailey."

"And his name?"

"Winnefrith. He has a crooked back. You can't miss him. Assuming you get into the upper bailey. Now, it's getting late. I have to be going."

Stephen and Gilbert left Rykelyng to finish dressing and went down to the garden. Bordered by the chapel, the chamber building and the hall, it had the look of an abbey cloister, crisscrossed by white gravel walkways between large bunches of rose bushes, which were bare. They crossed to the gate where they had a good view of the chapel doors.

The space before the main doors of the chapel had begun to fill up with people, all from the upper gentry in their fine clothes.

Stephen watched for a crooked-backed man. Surely, Giles' valet would come to pay his respects for his master. But no crooked-backed man could be seen.

"You can manage for a while, can't you?" Gilbert asked after a period of fruitless waiting. "I have need of the privy."

"I'll be all right," Stephen said.

Gilbert nodded and hurried into the chamber building, for they had detected the presence of a privy by the stench off the main door.

A hush fell over the crowd and all faces swung toward a procession coming round a corner of the chapel. It was King Henry. Stephen had never seen the king before, and was surprised at how ordinary and unimposing he looked. He was of average height and slender build. He wore a gold circlet upon wavy brown hair which fell to the shoulders. His face was squarish, a look accentuated by a beard trimmed to a square below his chin just as Rykelyng's. The mouth was small and framed by moustaches that had been allowed to grow out so they sagged around the corners. His brown eyes had a dog-like air, soft and friendly. The king smiled at this man and that, greeting many by name as he walked toward the chapel.

Edward came behind his father, towering over everyone with his great height and long legs, and just behind him was a dark-haired woman of great beauty. This had to be his wife, Leonor, since the woman Isabel Gascelyn followed her with three other ladies-in-waiting.

Behind the royal procession were a number of high-ranking men. Stephen recognized Gilbert de Clare, frowning and his eyes downcast, as if something was bothering him, and other barons and earls.

Beside de Clare was another man Stephen knew well, and wished he didn't, Percival FitzAllan, the earl of Arundel. There was bad blood between them. FitzAllan suspected — rightly — that Stephen had played a role in the burning of one of FitzAllan's castles by partisans of Simon de Montfort. And as a result, FitzAllan had tried to ruin Stephen with a cocked-up charge of murder.

But the greatest shock of all was the girl who followed FitzAllan: a small, pretty blonde girl of sixteen in an expensive blue silk gown with two hatchet-faced women on either side of her who hung close as if there was some danger that she might sprint away — Stephen's step-niece Ida. She was the last person he expected to see at Windsor Castle, and her presence made him uneasy.

FitzAllan had seized custody of her last year when Ida's mother claimed that Stephen's brother had adopted the girl and made her his heir, thus depriving Stephen of the inheritance of his home manor, Hafton.

The girl saw Stephen peering through the gate. Her blue eyes flashed with hope. Her lips moved: "Help me."

Then she disappeared into the chapel.

What was Ida doing here with FitzAllan?

The shock of seeing Ida left him stunned and unable to think, and the crowd had mostly gone into the chapel when Gilbert showed up at Stephen's elbow.

Gilbert looked anxiously at Stephen's face. "What's happened?"

"Ida's here. I saw her. With FitzAllan."

"Oh, goodness." Gilbert glanced at the chapel. "No sign of Elysande?" Elysande Attebrook was William's widow and Ida's mother.

"No. I would have expected her to be with Ida if she's here."

"You know what this means — he intends to press Elysande's suit before the king. The usual procedures of the law be damned."

"I suppose he does," Stephen said. Since Hafton was a crown manor granted to his family by the king, the matter could be disposed of in the crown court than by the king himself. In fact, in the usual run of things, someone of Elysande's stature could not expect to make an appeal directly to the king and get a ready hearing; she was a gentlewoman, but of the lower gentry like Stephen himself, and people that low could not count on gaining the king's attention. But FitzAllan, who was one of the realm's great men, might do so on her behalf. And how better to present the case than with the prospective heir dangled, a young marriageable girl, before the king?

If that was the case, it was not hard to guess how things would turn out. The king needed FitzAllan's support far more than he needed that of a little man like Stephen. FitzAllan, after all, could raise a hundred men or more for the king. So, the judgment was a foregone conclusion. He would remain a landless man with no income, facing poverty again when his money ran out. Then it would be back to the garret chamber at the Broken Shield Inn that he had inhabited when he first came to Ludlow.

When the crowd filed into the church, Stephen and Gilbert left the garden. They intended to enter the church and continue the search for Winnefrith, but guards at the door turned them away. The Mass would be for the nobility and well-connected alone.

The Mass went on for more than an hour.

At last, the king and the royal party emerged into the wan December daylight. The king headed uphill toward the upper bailey. The magnates and their retinues who were privileged to have access to the more refined precincts of the castle streamed after the king.

Stephen was about to follow the king when Prince Edward, his wife and her ladies-in-waiting came out of the church with a priest. They went toward the gate on the other side of the lower bailey.

"A private graveside service?" Gilbert guessed.

"That would explain the priest," Stephen said. "Since none came yesterday."

"Still no sign of Winnefrith," Gilbert said, peering around the jam of the gate. "Ah! Wait!"

Gilbert pointed to a stooped figure who had come out of the stable and trailed after the prince's party.

"Do we go after them?" Gilbert said.

"I think you know the answer to that," Stephen said, stepping out toward the gate.

He limped toward the gate, unable to move at his usual rapid pace, so Gilbert was able to keep up without trouble.

When they rounded the northwest corner of the castle, Edward's party was passing through the gate of the little chapel at the foot of the hill.

Stephen and Gilbert entered the yard and paused at a corner of the chapel, where they had a view of the graveyard behind it. The prince's party was standing with bowed heads as the priest spoke a funeral service over a tilled mound of earth.

"Do you see him?" Gilbert whispered.

Stephen leaned around the corner for a better look at the graveyard. "No," he whispered back.

Gilbert's stomach gurgled, and he put his hands upon it. "Shall we go?"

"Not yet."

"But there are no servants here, either," Gilbert said. "The dining hall is our best chance to find him."

"Let's go around to the other side," Stephen said as the graveside service ended and the prince turned away from the grave. He ducked back because the prince was leading his party this way. "Maybe he's there."

As he cleared the far corner, Gilbert bumped into a short man whose muscular right shoulder hung below his left. He had grey hair, well combed, and wore a blue cloak over a green wool coat and yellow stockings. His lined face said he was fifty if a day, and a flap of skin hung from the point of his chin to just above the collar bone. He rubbed that chin with a blunt-fingered hand where Gilbert's forehead had injured it.

"Let me pass," the stoop-shouldered man said to Gilbert.

"We would have a word with you," Gilbert said.

"What of it? I've nothing to say to you."

He stepped around Gilbert.

"You are Winnefrith?" Stephen asked, moving in his way.

"Who asks?"

"My name is Stephen Attebrook."

"Of course, you are." Winnefrith sighed deeply and put on a sad face. "You must excuse me. I am overcome with grief. I loved Father Giles. It is difficult to speak of him."

"I won't trouble you long," Stephen said.

"Must you trouble me at all, sir?"

"It is necessary."

"I won't be answering any questions."

Winnefrith stepped to go around Stephen, but Stephen grabbed him by the collar and pulled their heads together.

"You'll answer my questions," Stephen said.

Winnefrith tried to push Stephen. He was surprisingly strong, but Stephen shook him hard.

"All right, all right," Winnefrith said, not sounding cowed, though. "What do you want?"

Stephen released his grip. "How well did you know your master?"

"As well as any servant."

"Which means he had no secrets you didn't know."

"Well, I wouldn't say that."

"How long had you been in his service?"

"Nigh on fifteen years. He could have easily let me go, given my infirmity. As you see, I am not as hardy as I once was. But he kept me on."

"Did he have any enemies?"

"None. He was loved by everyone who knew him."

"What about debts?"

Winnefrith shook his head. "Father Giles had none, I'm sure of it. He had the living of four parishes and kept close attention to the accounts. He was never wanting for money."

"And he wasn't given to gambling?"

"Gracious, no! He thought that sinful."

"Nor to drinking and whores?"

Winnefrith's eyes shifted back and forth. "Well, he was a man, after all. What man doesn't fancy drink and women?"

"What was his relationship with Isabel Gascelyn?"

Winnefrith blinked. "None, sir! None other than he was her confessor!"

Stephen let silence reign for a few moments. "You're sure about that?"

"Positive, sir!" Winnefrith cried. "I cannot believe it! I refuse to believe it! Lady Isabel is a virtuous woman!"

"But Father Giles was not so virtuous?"

Winnefrith's eyes dropped. "I told you, he had a weakness for women."

"Whom else might he have been involved with recently, if not Lady Isabel?"

Winnefrith wrung his hands together. "I cannot say for certain."

"But you suspect someone."

"Well, I, er … yes."

"And you do not know her name."

"No, he did not confide her name to me. And I know that whatever the nature of the liaison, it ended. And not happily."

"Not happily for whom?"

"Father Giles, I'm afraid. He was sore depressed about it."

Stephen changed tacks. "Did he serve anyone else?"

"He also served the prince and his lady as their chaplain and confessor."

"The prince? Edward?"

"Of course. How many princes are there?"

Stephen took a few moments to consider his next question.

"You said that Father Giles had been depressed recently. Was that his mood the day he disappeared?"

"I cannot say it was," Winnefrith said.

"And how did you realize he had disappeared?"

"His bed was not slept in when I came to wake and dress him."

"And you sounded the alarm immediately?"

"I, well, I … I waited until dinner time."

"Why?"

"I thought he might have spent the night with his lady of interest," Winnefrith said heavily.

"And you're sure, as we stand here, that you don't know who that was?"

"No — I swear I do not! Put me to the test! I do not lie! Father Giles made a special point of not confiding matters of his heart to me — on account he did not want to risk embarrassing the lady in question should anyone overhear."

"A lady who might be married?"

Winnefrith sighed, and nodded.

When there was no question immediately forthcoming, he asked, "May I go now? Dinner should be underway."

Stephen nodded. Meals to a servant were an important matter. It was a significant part of their compensation, and if they were late for the common meal, they often got no more than scraps.

"Oh," he said, remembering something. "Why were only Father Giles' travel clothes out to laundry? Did he go somewhere?"

Winnefrith paused. "He went to London."

"How long was Father Giles in London?" Gilbert asked.

"A week," Winnefrith said.

"Do you remember the days — the precise day he left and the precise day he returned?"

Winnefrith frowned. "Why, he left five days before the Feast of Saint Nicholas and returned the day after."

Stephen considered this answer. It meant that Giles had gone to London on the first of December and returned on Friday, the 7th — the day before his disappearance.

"I take it you didn't go with him?" Stephen asked.

"No, he rode alone."

"Why did he go there?" Stephen asked.

"He went to see a friend, a Father Bernard, at Saint Paul's. They trained as priests together at Westminster Abbey. Father Bernard was Father Giles' confessor. My lord had something weighing on his mind and would see no one else about it. That's all I know."

"That's all for now," Stephen said. "We will, however, want to inspect his quarters. After dinner, of course. You'll be at the king's hall in the upper bailey?"

"Yes," Winnefrith said.

"We will await you there."

"Of course, sir." Winnefrith bowed and left the yard.

"Do you believe him?" Gilbert asked as they passed around behind the towering motte within the middle bailey to the next gate. "He seemed a bit shifty."

"Protecting the identity of the lady, no doubt," Stephen said.

"Yes, I agree with that. He knew."

"I wonder who she is," Stephen said.

"Do you think it a matter worth pursuing?"

"You don't think so?" Gilbert asked.

"Well, her husband would have a good motive for murder if he found out about the affair. Who would know about that better than the lady in question?"

"Who better," Gilbert agreed.

"But I think we already know who the lady is, though."

"Ah, yes," Gilbert said. "Lady Isabel."

"Obvious from the start, no? She wanted the cross as a keepsake. I'll wager it was her gift to him. She didn't want the chance of anyone seeing it and guessing that fact. He's covering for her."

"No leaping to conclusions there, when they are plain as day."

Stephen and Gilbert passed through the gate to the upper bailey, and Stephen asked directions to the king's hall.

One of the gate wardens pointed to a stone building with a blue tiled roof a short distance away. "There it is, sir," the warden said. "It's the one between the queen's chambers and the chapel. Just go round the queen's chamber to the garden. You can't miss it."

You couldn't miss it if you were familiar with the place. As a stranger, though, it might be easy to do so. But following the direction of the finger, Stephen and Gilbert entered the garden and approached a wide double doorway in a high stone building straight ahead. The muffled uproar of conversation and the singing of minstrels beat through the door, giving the place away.

"Ida's in there," Gilbert mused. "It would be nice to see her again. I hope she is well."

"She's in some sort of trouble," Stephen said. He suspected what that trouble might be, but it hurt even to think about it, much less talk about it aloud.

"Something other than being in the clutches of that terrible man?"

"It seems so."

Gilbert frowned. "You're not thinking about barging in, are you?"

"No," Stephen said. "Come, have faith. I am more clever than that."

"Sadly, you do not always give that impression." Gilbert sniffed the air which was scented with the aroma of fresh-baked bread. "A pity you've made me miss dinner."

"It is a sacrifice I am willing to make," Stephen said, disregarding the growling of his own stomach.

"But why am I always the one to make them?"

"Fasting is good for you."

"Only on fast days. This is not one of them."

"You wait here for Winnefrith," Stephen said. "FitzAllan's unlikely to remember you. I'm going to make myself scarce. He may not have heard the gossip about us being here."

"How likely do you really think that is?"

It was not likely at all, actually, but making himself scarce avoided the possibility of contention if FitzAllan or any of his following came out to the garden.

He said, "I'll be waiting at the gate."

"Are you sure you know the way?"

Gilbert and Winnefrith came for him half an hour later.

Winnefrith led them around the queen's chambers into the bailey, which was big enough for two ordinary castles of the kind inhabited by the average baron.

The chapel stood at a right angle to the hall and parallel to the north wall. A small door gave access the chapel, and Winnefrith led Stephen and Gilbert through it and up a spiral staircase to the immediate left. The staircase ended on the first floor where one passage opened onto a gallery overlooking the hall, through which voices could be heard in conversation — Edward arguing for some position that the king should take during an upcoming meeting with Montfort and the rebels to take place in a few weeks before King Louis of France. Stephen almost looked in to see who was there, but Winnefrith paused impatiently in the opening to the upper floor of the chapel.

Winnefrith went down a hallway, and stopped about halfway. He opened a door to one of the chambers.

"Here we are, sir," he said.

The room was dark and Stephen had to feel his way across it to open the shutters of the chamber's single window so they would have some light to work by.

"Will that be all, sir?" Winnefrith asked. "May I take my leave?"

"No," Stephen said. "I wish you to remain. As a witness to our search, so you can say nothing of value was taken."

"As you wish, sir," Winnefrith said stiffly.

The chamber was furnished with curtained bed, padded chair, wardrobe, side tables with legs carved to resemble vines curling around them, and a fireplace. The walls were whitewashed and painted with designs of more vines and colored flowers, red, yellow, and blue.

Stephen opened the wardrobe. Full-fledged priest's vestments hung on hooks alongside more ordinary robes for daily wear. Three sets of boots were lined up beneath them, all well-cleaned. One of them, more battered than the others, must be Giles' travel boots. Stephen went through all the pockets in all the robes and probed inside each boot in case there were articles hidden in them.

There was a smallish chest beside the boots. Stephen tried the lid. It was unlocked. He opened it, but the chest was empty.

"He kept his money here?" Stephen asked Winnefrith. "And his jewelry?"

"Yes."

"What happened to it?"

"It was taken into safekeeping."

"By whom?"

"Princess Leonor. Do you mind telling me, sir, why you are … why you are pawing through Father Giles' effects?"

"Looking for something."

"What could that be, sir?"

"Something important."

"But what could be of importance here? What could lead to whoever killed him?"

"I will know it when I see it."

Winnefrith did not seem convinced of that, but he was obviously anxious about Stephen's invasion of Father Giles' private space.

Gilbert paid no heed to this conversation. His attention was taken up by a writing box on a table by the window. He opened the slanted lid.

"Nothing here," he said.

There was, however, a leather case on the floor by the table, the sort often used for storing documents. Gilbert knelt and flipped it open.

"Letters," Gilbert said. "Mainly to and from someone named Robert."

"That would be Father Giles' brother," Winnefrith said. "The Baron of Tottlesby."

"Never heard of it," Gilbert said.

"It's in the north. Yorkshire."

"Are you from there?" Gilbert asked, not taking his eyes off the letter. "I thought I heard Yorkshire in your speech. Though it is only a trace."

"I was born there," Winnefrith said. "I was away for years, though, and I guess that changes a man. I was in Gascony fighting for the king," he added with some pride and then bitterness crept into his voice. "I was not always like this. Once I stood straight as an oak. I was strong and able. But as

I grew older, something afflicted me. I have to be careful, for my bones break easily now."

"When did you first start to suffer from your affliction?" Stephen said, feeling under the pillows like a common burglar.

"Twenty years or so ago," Winnefrith said. "I fell from a horse, and was unnaturally slow to heal."

"And the family did not discharge you?" Stephen asked. So often, the crippled were cast aside. No one liked to be reminded of how frail their bodies were: there but for the grace of God, people often thought as they passed by the disabled and the halt and pretended they were not there. Once, Stephen might have felt the same way, but something had caused him to feel more sympathy for the afflicted.

"His father kept me on, God rest his soul," Winnefrith said. "Why?"

It was prying to ask about such things, and it was clear Winnefrith did not want this tack to continue.

"Oh, it's nothing," Stephen said, straightening up from the bed. "What did you do?"

"I was made valet to Father Giles. He was but a boy then."

Stephen put the pillows back in place, thinking now about turning over the mattress before he pulled the wardrobe out from the wall.

"What will you do now?" Stephen asked.

"The princess has kindly taken me into her household. I shall not want for work or a meal."

"That is fortunate."

Gilbert set down the letters and held a folio of vellum to the light coming through the window, his breath curling from his nostrils.

"What is that, Gilbert?" Stephen asked. "Have you found something?"

"I don't know," Gilbert replied, holding out the vellum sheet. "But have a look at this. It's a bill of sale for horses in London. It's dated the day of the feast of Saint Nicholas. He paid quite a lot for them, too."

Stephen accepted the vellum sheet. It showed that not only did Giles buy two horses, but the sale included bridles, saddle pads and saddles for them.

"Why would Father Giles buy a pair of horses in London?" Stephen asked Winnefrith.

Winnefrith looked startled. "I did not know he had bought any. He had no need. He already had three."

"And did he come back with these horses?"

"No," Winnefrith said. "He didn't."

Stephen rolled up the bill of sale and put it in his pouch.

"I think we're done here," he said.

Winnefrith looked relieved until Stephen added, "Winnefrith, I need one more service from you, if you would be so kind."

"Oh?" Winnefrith sounded doubtful.

"There is a young woman in the earl of Arundel's party. Do you think you can carry a message to her from me?"

"I will try."

"Her name is Ida Attebrook. Ask her to meet me in the chapel below us. But only if she can manage it alone. Don't let anyone overhear the request."

"Ah," Winnefrith murmured.

"She's my niece," Stephen said to dispel any suspicions Winnefrith might have. "I want to talk about family matters with her out of earshot of her minders."

"I think I might be able to manage, sir," Winnefrith said.

"Thank you. I appreciate it."

The chapel was dark but for thin blades of sunlight coming through the gaps in the shutters over its many windows. Stephen sat behind one of the stone columns that marched in parallel down the length of the chamber, dividing it into thirds. It was hushed and peaceful, or would have been so except for his worrying about Ida.

Time ticked by, what must be an hour or more, at least. He had about given up hope that she would come, when the door at the other end of the chapel opened, spilling sunlight into the dimness. A woman's figure was silhouetted in that light.

He heard the scrape of shoe leather on a stone floor: only one pair of feet. She had been able come alone after all, Stephen thought with relief. He had been worried that even in the confines of the bailey she would be under the thumbs of her minders. He climbed to his feet, experiencing an unexpected rush of pleasure at the prospect of seeing her.

"Stephen?" Ida whispered. "Are you there?"

He stepped into the middle aisle. "Here, Ida."

She ran toward him and leaped up to grasp him around the neck. The force of her dash staggered him back a few feet. His arms went around her waist, so that her feet dangled in the air. He felt tears upon her cheek before he set her down.

"Dear God," she said, laying her forehead against his chest. "I am so glad to see you."

"And I you." Stephen wanted to ask her about her plea for help, but his mind was a jumble of feelings. He managed to stammer, "Are you safe? Are you well?"

"Well enough, if you count being fed regularly and given a soft bed. There isn't much to occupy the mind when you're a prisoner. Not even a single book to be had anywhere in Clun. And safe? FitzAllan hasn't threatened my life, but he's said he might have me beaten until I come round to his notions."

"And what notions are those?"

"He intends to seek the king's leave to hold me as his ward."

"You don't think that was obvious the moment FitzAllan had you carried off?" Stephen asked softly. He had known this in his bones, but hadn't wanted to confront the thought. The places where it led were too painful to think about.

"Can't you fight it?"

"I don't know what I can do to change matters. The manor is held of the king. He is the final appeal in any challenge to seisin. You know what the outcome of a contest between FitzAllan and me will be in that court."

"You know what power comes with a wardship," Ida said bitterly. "The power to choose a husband!"

"Yes," Stephen murmured. He recalled Rykelyng's remark about coming into his estate through his marriage to an heiress. That woman would have been just such a ward as Ida. Such women, particularly the rich ones, were reckoned to be great prizes and were much sought after. Lords bought the loyalty of their men with the gift of such prizes. The wishes of the women counted for nothing.

"Then you can guess what happens now. FitzAllan wants me wed to one of his men. An odious spider of a man without lands of his own. I'd sooner die than be his wife."

Ida drew a breath and let it out.

"You have to stop it somehow."

Chapter 5

"We need to find the writing office," Stephen said to Gilbert as they waited in the chapel doorway for Ida to make her way across the upper bailey to her quarters in one of the timber buildings leaning against the castle's south wall. "I need to write a letter. It's probably the only place close by with parchment and quills."

"You want to write a letter?" Gilbert asked. "Whatever for?"

"We need to tell the prince we're leaving for London tomorrow." Stephen had been in hot water once before for failing to keep a superior advised of his actions in an investigation and he wasn't about to risk such a thing happening again.

Gilbert considered this; it was the first time Stephen had broached what their next move would be. "Shouldn't we pursue the matter of Lady Isabel's involvement, and that of her husband? Instead of running around the countryside chasing who knows what of a dead end?"

"Lady Isabel isn't going anywhere she can't be found," Stephen said grimly. "We have other matters to take care of first."

"And what could those matters be?" Gilbert asked.

Stephen glared at Gilbert and did not reply.

Gilbert's mouth opened and shut. He nodded slowly. "Oh, of course. I see. London. Away from here. But it's an excuse, surely."

"Right. One that will be believed. That's all we need to explain our absence."

Gilbert paced a step or two as the thought of what they were about to do and the special dangers it posed sank in. "Why not just tell the prince in person?" he asked, returning to the subject of the letter.

"He could object."

"Do you really suppose he would?"

"He might find a trip to London a wild-goose chase. And if not him, someone close to him might. And then we'd never get there."

"It is probably a wild-goose chase," Gilbert lamented. "Except for ..." he glanced around as if to see if there was anyone close enough to overhear, and even though there wasn't, he did not go on. "But still! The prince wants an answer in a week. How can we give it to him in that time if we spent the bulk of it away?"

"Then we must get busy. Standing around here and debating about what to do doesn't get it done. Ida's in. Let's go."

Gilbert caught Stephen's arm. "Do you think it's a good idea to be seen coming out of the chapel even after she has gone in?"

"You're right." Stephen nodded toward the door to the queen's chamber block. "We'll pass through here to the hall and out to the cloister."

Writing materials were not common. Clerks of magnates had them, of course. But Stephen didn't feel comfortable approaching just any clerk and asking to borrow parchment and quill.

There was a place, however, where such implements could be found in abundance, and where it was not unusual for strange people to come and go on errands that were not questioned.

The office of the Clerk of the King's Chamber was in a stone building on the other side of the hall. It was tall and built of stone, unlike all but the king's hall and chambers, and the chapel, with a blue tiled roof, dignified as befitted its purpose as the beating heart of the king's administration. For here all the king's writs were copied and logged before being dispatched either to the Chancery at Westminster for reproduction and sealing with the Great Seal or to designated recipients by the messengers who loitered around the fireplace on the ground floor, awaiting instructions.

Stephen and Gilbert climbed to the first floor. The writing office took up the entire chamber, which was high, long and narrow. Two tables parallel to each other ran the length of the room, where a dozen tonsured clerics sat scribbling away, their fingers stained with black ink; some had smudges on their faces where the fingers had rubbed them, especially around the eyes and upon the bridges of noses.

There were three tables in the middle of these two long ones and at right angles to them. At the far end, was the senior clerk's table, so that he could preside over the operations of all the others. The middle table and the one at Stephen's end were occupied by the clerks responsible for different departments. One department specialized in legal writs and general correspondence, one in those directed to sheriffs, and another in charge of foreign correspondence.

Whenever the king took himself to another place, the entire apparatus usually went with him. Without the writing office, the king could not make his will known to his subjects.

Stephen surveyed the room from the doorway. There was some murmured conversation, but the scratching of quill pens was the most predominant sound, a nervous sort of thing.

The clerk directly ahead was slumped in his chair, chin on his chest, contributing to the murmur with a gentle snore. No one paid Stephen the slightest attention.

He slipped onto a stool beside the sleeping clerk, and extracted a fragment of vellum that had been scraped clean of its writing from beneath several draft letters. He plucked a quill pen from the sleeping clerk's fist and, sliding the clerk's ink pot over, dipped the pen and started to write hastily but in as good a clerk's hand as he could manage, given the pressure to finish quickly before someone could interfere.

Stephen finished the letter, which he set aside, and tugged a second piece of vellum from the pile of drafts. This was the important message, and the one he had really come to write in secret. It was a short message, only a few words, and was quickly finished, too. He returned the pen to the clerk's hand. The clerk snorted and his chest heaved.

Stephen retreated to the stairwell, forcing himself to walk calmly as if he belonged there. The vellums lay on the palms of his hands while he blew on the ink to dry it.

"I thought surely that fellow would wake up!" Gilbert said. "Imagine what would have happened if he had!"

"I'd have said something clever, he'd laugh, and that would be the end of it."

The ink was stubborn. It was not drying as rapidly as Stephen hoped. Carrying it any distance before it had dried risked the ink smearing and running. He opened the shutter of the narrow window in the stairwell and lay the letters on the sill in the expectation that the fresh air would hasten the process.

The pause provided the chance to view the buildings along the east and south walls of the bailey. They were the typical structures you found in castles, timber-framed and three stories high with slate roofs and the newest of household amenities, chimneys for fireplaces, three to a structure. Unlike some castle buildings, though, these seemed to have no cellars, nor were the ground floors in stone. Perhaps this was because they were used as apartments rather than for storage.

His eye wandered across those on the east wall, then stopped and shot back. He'd seen something there that was out of place. It took some time to find it again. It was what appeared from this distance to be an entrance to a cellar for the top of the opening in the side of the building was only about three feet off the ground and there appeared to be stairs leading down to it. There was another odd thing about this door. Paths led to all the doors along the walls except for this one. If it was a cellar, it was not much used. What was the point to a cellar if you didn't use it?

Stephen checked to see if the ink was dry at last. It was. He folded up the vellum strips and put them in his pouch.

"I wonder," he said to himself as he started down the circular staircase.

"You wonder?" Gilbert asked. "What about?"

"Come on," Stephen said.

He took the stairs two at a time, heedless of the pain this caused his sprained ankle. Once outside, he set off briskly toward this mysterious doorway.

Gilbert caught up halfway across the bailey. "Have you lost your mind? FitzAllan's people might see us!"

"Can't be helped," Stephen said as he limped to the peculiar doorway.

But Gilbert's caution caused him to study the apartments along the south wall, where Ida's and FitzAllan's apartments were located. The windows were shuttered against the cold weather.

"Nothing to worry about," Stephen said. "Nobody's seen us."

"Why are we standing before someone's cellar?" Gilbert asked.

"I don't think this leads to a cellar."

"Looks like a cellar to me."

"If it was a cellar, why wouldn't it be in use?"

"What are you talking about?"

"Look there. There should be a path." Stephen pointed to the top of the stairway where the grass was almost knee high and a happy green despite the season. There was no path.

"What else could it be but a cellar, anyway?"

"I have an idea," Stephen said, starting down the stairs.

They ended about ten feet under the surface at a thick oak door. Stephen tried the latch. It was not locked. He opened the door and stepped into the darkness beyond it.

"What is this?" Gilbert asked uncertainly behind him.

"I think it's a sally port," Stephen said.

"It runs beneath the wall?"

"You are on top of your game today," Stephen grinned. "Come on. Mind your head."

Gilbert didn't need to mind his head as much as Stephen did, for the tunnel that stretched ahead was just high enough to let him stand upright. He didn't trust the builder, though, and ran a hand along the roof overhead as well as along a wall as he shuffled on an uneven surface into a gloom so thick that he could not see his feet after some distance. The air was dank and smelled of piss.

Eventually, he bumped into another oak door. This too was not locked. He opened it and tripped on a set of stairs on the other side, narrowly avoiding bashing his head on them when he fell forward. The steps led up to a third door. Stephen felt about for the door handle and the lock that had to be securing the door. He found the handle but no lock. He lifted the handle. The door opened a crack, sending a thin shaft of faint light across his shoulder and upon the stairs.

"Ah, ha!" Stephen said.

"What is it?" Gilbert asked.

"The answer to a prayer I haven't even made yet."

A courtyard, especially a courtyard barren in winter, was not a good place to remain inconspicuous. The hedges provided some cover, but they had been trimmed down, so if Gilbert wished to be unseen by members of the FitzAllan party, he would have to lie on his ample belly, and that would not have done. Someone would notice, come over to see what he was doing, and inevitably conclude that he had no business here.

And yet people came and went while Gilbert lingered under one of the many apple trees planted in the courtyard and no one paid him much attention. Curious that. He nervously wondered why that was so, if the upper bailey was the province of the noble born and those who served them, a place to relax away from the unwashed commons. Perhaps that was it; he was mistaken as a servant, although he wore no noble's livery, the usual costume for servants of the rich.

Stephen had given him a simple task: get word to Ida to find a way to leave the hall later in the evening. But Gilbert still wasn't sure how he was to do that. He had come up with and discarded numerous plans as the sun sank behind the walls, casting the courtyard in shadow. And he had yet to fashion one that was satisfactory.

Foot traffic increased through the yard as the wealthy who were entitled to supper with the king made their way to the great hall.

Gilbert nervously watched them for signs he had been detected and for Ida. Fortunately for his galloping heart, he hadn't been noticed yet. It seemed only a matter of time.

Meanwhile, there was no sign of Ida, either.

He began to worry that the FitzAllan party was not coming. Had FitzAllan concluded his business over custody of Hafton Manor and its presumed heiress?

However, at last, FitzAllan made his appearance. His close-cropped hair — an odd fashion followed by no one else Gilbert could think of — and his large head on massive shoulders made the earl a hard man to miss.

He was surrounded by at least twenty retainers, male and female, and at first Gilbert did not spot Ida. But there she was, in the midst of a gaggle of women, with her two maids at her heels. He had hoped he would not find her among a crowd!

Gilbert came away from his tree as FitzAllan passed close with the thought of blundering into Ida or something, risking a beating to pass his message: a strip of vellum wrapped about a stone.

But they went by before Gilbert could rouse his courage to make the attempt, and were gone inside the hall.

He had failed!

Everything — Ida's life and future, the desperate plan Stephen had fashioned — had depended on him, and he had been too frightened to act!

He could not face Stephen.

The Corpse at Windsor Bridge

Gilbert wandered through the chapel to the bailey, his mind churning. A breath of wind brought the aromas of a kitchen behind the building housing the writing office, and the glimmer of a glimpse of an idea began forming in his mind.

He went round the writing office to the courtyard where a kitchen stood against the north wall. A parade of servants was tracking to the hall bearing full trays while others brought back the empty ones. The hurry and bustle made him think of a line of ants going to and from their hill.

The wide double doors to the kitchen remained open to admit this ant race of servants. Gilbert watched them for a few moments, and then got in line and went in boldly as if he belonged there.

Just within the doorway was a cloak room where cloaks and coats hung from pegs. A thin fellow was removing his cloak and coat, and putting it up as Gilbert stood in the doorway. The thin man passed around him and entered the kitchen: one of the cooks?

Gilbert noted that some of the coats were like those worn by the servants going and coming at that hall.

He searched through these coats for one that would fit. Most seemed far too small, but at last he located one that seemed alright. It was just alright: it was tight across the shoulders and he managed to fasten the buttons, but, looking down, the fabric between them was strained apart and revealed his linen shirt. It would have to do.

Back in the kitchen, he took up a pitcher which he filled with wine in the buttery, and marched off with the procession toward the hall.

The way through involved several twists and turns, but then Gilbert burst forth into the hall proper. He nearly froze in his tracks at the stunning magnificence of the scene. Only the pressure of the servants behind him kept his feet moving. While the others fanned out among the tables, Gilbert edged against a dark paneled wall so overcome that he could barely breathe, much less move.

The hall, like all halls, was much longer than it was wide, but there the resemblance to an ordinary hall faded to nothingness. Around all the walls to a height greater than that of a man, lush, dark wood panels covered the bare stone. It would have been enough just to display those panels, but almost the entire circumference of them was covered by thick tapestries of all sorts of scenes depicted in brilliant colors — hunting, jousting, battle scrums, peaceful orchards with beautiful rich women strolling among the trees and flowers, a large snow-covered mountain with small figures climbing a path to the top.

Above the panels and tapestries, large, glass-filled windows admitted the best light you could find in a hall so that rather than being dingy, a frequent condition of the ordinary hall, this one was filled with natural light even though sundown was not far off. And those windows — some were of clear glass, some of green, some of red, and a few of the windows held scenes made of colored glass as you would find in cathedrals.

Three lines of tables marched in parallel down the middle of the hall to the king's high table, which sat crosswise in front of a massive fireplace that burned high and might have roasted the backsides of those at the high table if they had not been seated in high-backed chairs.

The king was there in the middle with the queen. He was speaking to a woman on the other side of the queen. The woman and the queen laughed in what seemed a rather forced way as if they did not actually find what the king had to say to be that amusing; Gilbert approved of a practice of laughing at a king's jokes even if they weren't funny.

"Don't just stand there, you idiot!" someone hissed in Gilbert's ear. "Get to work, damn it!"

"Right away!" Gilbert sputtered.

He left the protection of the wall and moved among the tables. Here and there, revelers held out their cups for him to fill them as he made his way in the direction opposite of the high table. He had seen the Earl of Arundel at the king's table, but no sign of Ida in that direction. Although she came from a gentle family, it was a modest one, and Gilbert guessed he would probably find her near the far wall.

He came to her about two-thirds of the way down. Her back was to him, but she noticed him when she turned her head to speak to the woman beside her, one of her maids. Ida's eyes widened, and she looked down, hastily composing her face.

Gilbert paused at Ida's shoulder. "Ah, my lady, more wine?"

"Yes, thank you," Ida said.

She started to raise her cup, but Gilbert motioned for her to put it down by her trencher.

Gilbert bent over Ida to pour and as he did so, dropped the little stone with its message in Ida's lap. She covered it quickly with her skirt.

"I'll have more, too," the maid beside Ida said, waving toward her own cup.

"Of course," Gilbert said. Fortunately, he still had a bit left, though not enough to fill the cup. "I am all out, I'm afraid, my lady. I shall be right back!"

He fled the hall quickly but with as dignified a step as he could manage.

Stephen kept watch over the dark courtyard from the shelter of the chapel doorway.

After some time, a woman emerged from the hall. She paused and looked around. The woman crossed to a bench along one of the graveled paths and sat down.

Stephen stepped out of the doorway, guessing that had to be Ida. But then the door to the hall opened again and another woman came out. She spotted the woman on the bench and went to her.

"My lady," the second woman said. "Are you all right?"

"Something I ate hasn't agreed with me," the first woman said.

Stephen's heart thudded. It was Ida.

"I am feeling rather ill," Ida said.

"Should I summon a physician?"

"No. I just feel nauseous, is all. I think I'll be all right soon. But I didn't want to embarrass myself inside, if you know what I mean."

"Of course. Are you sure you don't want me to stay with you?"

"I see no reason. Go. Enjoy the spectacle. You're not likely to see anything like it again."

"Surely not," the second woman agreed. She patted Ida's shoulder and went back into the hall.

Stephen counted to three and walked up to Ida. She rose as she spotted him.

"What is it?" Ida asked.

"We have to go now. It's our only chance."

"Go?" Ida asked as they crossed the outer bailey to the sally port stairwell. "Go where?"

"Away from here."

"But where?"

"London, for now. I know a place where you will be safe for a while, at least."

"London," she murmured. "I hear that it's grand. I never thought I'd see it."

"It's grand, all right, and dangerous enough in its own right. But it's all I can think to do for you at the moment."

Ida grasped his hand as they reached the stairwell. "So, you are kidnapping me. Stealing me away."

"Yes. I am."

She squeezed Stephen's hand. "I rather like that."

It was odd to hear the pleasure in her voice at the prospect of kidnapping. She had been kidnapped last summer by men whose purpose was far more sinister than Stephen's was now, and she had suffered greatly for it.

"Let's hope you don't come to change your mind about it," Stephen said.

They reached the bottom of the stairs. Stephen opened the first door and they went in. He thought he heard whispers that fell silent as the door scraped open. Was someone else here? He waited and heard nothing further. He had come too far already, though, to stop now. Feeling his way along one wall with one hand, he drew Ida after him with the other.

Some way in, Stephen tripped and fell on an object in his path. The object proved to be a man and a woman. She shrieked and the man bellowed.

Stephen scrambled to his feet. "Sorry, sorry. No harm meant. We've the same idea as you. Can we pass?"

He heard the pair edge out of the way.

"God's toenails, man," the woman complained. "I think you've broken my ribs."

Stephen recovered Ida's hand and they stepped around the couple. "Sorry about the ribs. I wouldn't want your husband to find out what you've been up to."

"I'll be after you if they are broken," the woman growled.

After they had retreated some distance, Ida whispered, "Do you think they'll say anything?"

"I doubt it. They don't want to be found out any more than we do."

At last, they reached the far stairs and climbed upward.

Stephen felt for the door latch, and opened the door to a rush of cold air.

"Come on," he said to Ida, taking her hand again.

They came up on the far side of the castle ditch in a stand of hazel.

Gilbert, mounted on his mule with Stephen's mare in tow, was some distance away, but he saw them and eased the mule forward.

Gilbert slid off the mule. "We should not tarry."

Stephen mounted the mare and held out a hand for Ida, who would have to ride behind him. Gilbert helped her up, and mounted the mule. Ida put her arms around Stephen's waist and lay her head against his back.

"Are you warm enough?" Stephen asked. "I've extra blankets if you need one."

"I'm fine," she said.

A three-quarter waning moon had just begun to rise, providing some illumination through scattered clouds for the ride through the chill night. They went north first, toward a farm path that led to the Thames and along it later to the Stanes bridge five or six miles away to the southeast.

Chapter 6

The streets of London were always crowded with people bustling about their business. Sundays were no exception, and when the traveling party arrived in London through Ludgate, the pace of their progress slowed to a crawl.

They skipped some of the congestion by taking a path crossing before the ruins of old Montfichet Castle, which was a ruin that had been much plundered of its stone so that the remains of walls looked as though they had been gnawed on by giant rats; squatters living in the rubble watched them pass with suspicious eyes.

When they met Carters Street on the other side of the castle, Stephen kept south by a monastery until the road ended at the Watergate, where he picked up Thames Street. This street was more crowded than any of the others they had traversed, for this infamous street was the home of many taverns, brothels, gambling dens and inns, where lives and fortunes were frittered away.

At the Queenhuthe, one of the city's many wharves, Stephen turned up a lane and stopped in front of a large house which had a yellow ribbon tacked to the door frame.

Ida slid off the mare and waited with her hands on her hips for Stephen to dismount.

"This is it?" she asked. "This is our destination? You've brought us to a whorehouse?" She sounded amused rather than shocked.

"I, well …"

"So, you think so little of me that you'd have me consort with low women?"

"I, uh, maybe, I'm afraid. Only for a short time."

"You surprise me so, Stephen. I'd not thought you frequented such places."

"I had a dissolute youth. Ask Gilbert. He knows all about it. And what he doesn't know, he's willing to imagine."

"He hasn't recovered yet from it," Gilbert said, rubbing his backside then stretching. "What are we doing here, anyway? You weren't thinking of taking rooms here. That inn we stayed in last time was so nice."

"Not exactly." Stephen added, "You may not be aware of this, but all the inns are required to report the names of guests to their ward aldermen. The same requirement does not apply to brothels."

"I see," Ida said. "How clever of you."

"It will have to do, I hope," he said.

Stephen mounted low steps and entered the front room with Ida and Gilbert at his heels.

Two girls at a table in the hall saw him. One said, "Ellie! Your turn!"

"Is Maggie here?" Stephen asked.

"Maggie?" Ellie asked, rising from the table. She blinked in surprise at Ida, and asked, "What do you want with her?"

"A word."

"Ah, come on. A stout brawny fellow like you'll want more than a word, and she's not the one to give it to you." She rubbed a breast against Stephen's arm, with a wink at Ida. "Nice and soft, can't you see? They can be yours for a whole hour. We could even make it a threesome with your friend here."

"I'll settle for the word with Maggie."

"You're no fun." Ellie pouted. The expression seemed forced, as her offers of pleasure had been.

"I am afraid so. Now go fetch her, if you please."

With some relief, Ellie climbed the stairs, bawling for Maggie.

Maggie descended the stairs a short while later. "I remember you. you're the Attebrook boy. What in the great toad are you doing here?"

"I need a favor."

"It is … it is — unseemly!" Maggie said when Stephen finished talking. "A lady like this? Hiding in my house?"

"Well," Stephen said, surprised that a woman of Maggie's profession would be struck by a sudden need to keep up appearances, "it won't be for long."

He glanced at Ida to gauge her reaction. Her expression was guarded, her arms crossed. Her eyes were on the hall, where a girl with her bodice open was having a nipple sucked by a customer. Her mouth curled in what might be taken as wry amusement or distaste. Stephen found he didn't know her well enough to tell which it was, and he was sorry he hadn't prepared her on the way for this. If she objected, which she well could and no one would blame her, he'd have to think of something else. Put her up at an inn? He was running out of money and doubted he could afford it for more than a few days. And she needed to stay hidden longer than that.

"She will not fit in!" Maggie protested. "She will stand out like a wart on the queen's arse. The ward will be all over me when the bailiffs find out she is here!"

So that was really it — not the impropriety of sheltering a gentlewoman but the trouble it might cause with the ward authorities, who were responsible for maintaining the moral tone of the area.

"Well, maybe not that much," Stephen said. "Have her keep to her chamber."

"Stephen, you are so kind to me," Ida said dryly. "How long were you thinking I should be on house arrest?"

"No more than a week or two. Only as long as it takes to clear up some business for Prince Edward."

"I wonder if I did the right thing, allowing you to carry me off," Ida said.

"He carried you off?" Maggie asked.

"Yes, kidnapped me," Ida said.

"Then there is no doubt," Maggie said. "You cannot stay. I will not be a party to such a thing."

"I jest," Ida said. "I'm on the run from a horrible man who wants to force me to marry him. Stephen is my uncle. He's protecting me from that terrible fate."

"I see," Maggie said. "Who is this monster who wants to wed you?"

"A greedy fellow from the March," Ida said. "But of course, you know it's my fortune he really wants, not my body."

"A fortune and a body to go with it. He would be a lucky man if he gets hold of you," Maggie said.

"So, you can see, the brute will never think to seek me here," Ida said. "And it will be only for a few days, until Stephen comes up with a better plan, right, Stephen?"

"That was the thought," Stephen said. He was embarrassed and certain that he'd made a terrible decision. Yet Maggie was, oddly, the only person he knew in London that he might be able to depend on. All the others had friends who had friends who knew FitzAllan, and if they knew the truth about Ida's situation — gossip had a habit of flying long distances — they were likely to seek FitzAllan's favor by turning her over to him. Maggie would do it for the money, but it would take her more time to figure things out. By then, Ida should be gone.

"As to standing out," Ida said, "I won't so much if I have another gown. Something more simple and suitable to this place."

"We can manage that," Maggie said.

"How much?" Stephen asked.

"For two weeks and a fresh gown?" Maggie replied. "A shilling should do it."

Stephen motioned for Gilbert, who poured out a shilling from the money bag.

Gilbert dumped twelve pence into Maggie's apron. She reached out a free hand to Ida.

"Will you come with me, Ida?" Maggie said. "I am sorry to be so familiar, but it seems wrong to call you 'my lady' if you're living here."

"Oh, that is quite all right," Ida said.

Maggie pointed to Ida's left hand. There was a gold ring set with a red stone on her first finger. "Be that a ruby?"

"It is," Ida said. "A present from my mother."

"You might also want to keep it out of sight. Don't want to tempt thieves. They're thicker around here than lice on a man's head. Or questions, for that matter."

"Of course." Ida removed the ring and dropped it in her purse.

"Let me show you to your room. You should find it quite comfortable, although it can get noisy at times. You understand."

They set off toward the back of the house.

Stephen heard Maggie ask, "Would it be an offense to ask if you are willing to help out around the house?"

"That depends on what you need," Ida said.

"Well, there are chamber pots that need emptying and laundry. There's no end to the laundry." Maggie smiled slyly.

"You know I will draw the line at that. However, I can read and write and cipher. Perhaps I can help keep your accounts."

Maggie looked astonished. "You can?"

"Of course. I had a tutor. He was very good. And my parents taught me how to examine accounts."

"I would be happy if you looked them over. I think the old fart who's doing the work now is cheating me."

Chapter 7

Since they had to be in London, it made sense to seek out this Father Bernard at Saint Paul's Cathedral, and find out what he knew about Father Giles' last days. It would be one dead end eliminated. And it was through the elimination of dead ends that murders were solved. Besides, it was Stephen's excuse for coming here.

Cathedrals were enormous places, and not just in terms of the central building itself. They were the seats of bishops who presided over a diocese, which could be as extensive and broad a land as that under the control of an earl, and the bishop of London, a man named Henry of Sandwich, needed a large staff consisting of archdeacons, subdeacons, deans, priests, bailiffs, stewards, and a horde of clerks to run his domain. Father Bernard was somewhere among this mob, if Winnefrith could be trusted, but finding him might not be that easy.

The cathedral close was rather like a fortress, with a high stone wall all around the complex. The main gate was at the end of Ludgate Street, and a short walk from the Brittany Inn, where Stephen and Gilbert had taken a chamber Sunday evening after Ida's accommodations had been arranged.

The following morning, Stephen and Gilbert followed a wagon filled with large stone blocks through the main gate.

The wagon rumbled away toward the spot where scaffolds could be seen against the cathedral's walls, its cargo meant either for repairs or a building project.

Stephen turned from watching the progress of the wagon and the activity upon the scaffolds to the porter manning the gate.

The porter noticed he was being looked at. He rubbed a pockmarked nose, and asked, "Can I help you, sir?"

"I'm looking for Father Bernard."

"And which Father Bernard would that be? Father Bernards are as common as goats around here."

"I'm not sure," Stephen said.

"Then you are in a pickle," the porter chuckled. "It will take you all day to chase them down. They're all over the place."

"The one I'm looking for should be rather young," Stephen said. "No more than twenty-five or so. And very well off."

"Ah, that would be Father Bernard le Erl. Not his real name, though. He's called that on account of the fact that his cousin's an earl. De Quincy's the family name."

De Quincy? Stephen ran that name around his tongue. He'd heard it before. Then it came to him: Robert de Quincy was earl of Winchester. This made Father Bernard a well-connected fellow.

"Where can I find him?" Stephen asked.

The porter gestured southward. "Over there at the Deanery. He's a subdeacon. An important man, hereabouts, and he's never shy about letting you know it. He's going places, that one. He'll be a bishop himself before you can shake a stick at him."

The Deanery was a large stone building on the south side of the cathedral close that sat within a courtyard surrounded by timber structures that appeared to be apartments.

It was such an important place that it had its own doorkeeper, who would not admit them far beyond the threshold. Apparently ordinary people were not allowed to wander in and out of the Deanery and disturb its important work. It was, after all, one of the main administrative centers of the diocese.

The doorkeeper sent a boy upstairs to announce Stephen and Gilbert's presence and settled on his stool to watch the shadows pass along the floor.

Presently, the boy returned. "Father Bernard will see you."

He took Stephen and Gilbert up the stairs to a chamber on a southern corner of the building where the windows stood open despite the weather to admit the sunlight. There were tables near these windows where clerks were scribbling away.

A young tonsured man sat on a highbacked chair with an embroidered blanket over his legs for warmth and what looked like a book of accounts on his lap. Stephen and Gilbert followed the boy to this young man; he introduced them and withdrew.

"Please sit down," Father Bernard said. He indicated a bench to his left. He was a tall man of about twenty-five, as Stephen expected, with light brown hair that fell in curls from his tonsure about a high forehead, amiable eyes and mouth, and chiseled cheeks and chin. Altogether he was a strikingly handsome man.

"What can I do for you?" Father Bernard continued.

"Are you the Father Bernard who is a friend to Father Giles de Twet?" Stephen asked.

"I am," Father Bernard said, frowning slightly. "We were acolytes together and took our vows at the same time. Why do you ask?"

Stephen sighed. "There's no way of softening the blow. But your friend has died."

If Stephen expected Bernard to suffer an outburst of grief, he was disappointed. Bernard frowned and pursed his mouth in thought.

"How did this happen?" Father Bernard asked.

"His body was found a few days ago in the Thames. It had been there two weeks."

"Foul play?"

"We suspect so."

"Two weeks, you say?"

"Just after he returned to Windsor from London."

"Ah."

"Do you have any idea why he came to London?"

"What is your interest?"

"Prince Edward has asked me to find his killer."

Father Bernard ran long fingers on the arm of his chair. "Giles did come to see me."

Stephen waited to see if Bernard would elaborate, but he did not.

"For what purpose?" Stephen asked.

"I took his confession."

"It is odd that he came all the way from Windsor for that, when he could have had it done there."

Bernard was silent for a few heartbeats. "He was troubled. The matter was difficult for him." He sighed. "I don't think he trusted anyone else. It was a highly sensitive matter. *Very* sensitive."

"Troubled you say. What, exactly, was his mood?"

Again there was a long pause. "Desperate, I would say."

"And you can't tell us what this matter was?"

"Of course, not."

"He did not seek your counsel outside of the confessional?" Stephen asked.

Bernard did not speak. The tip of his tongue touched his upper lip and withdrew.

"He did, didn't he," Stephen said.

"I cannot speak of it," Bernard said. "Lives hang in the balance."

"Not merely Giles'?"

"Not merely Giles'."

"The knowledge may help us find who killed him," Stephen urged.

"I cannot." Bernard shook his head; the curls rocked back and forth. "I will not."

Stephen waited a moment to see if Bernard would change his mind. When Bernard remained silent, he stood up.

"I see," Stephen said.

Bernard looked up at Stephen, eyes anguished. "I do not know you," he said. "I do not know what you would do with the knowledge."

"I suppose you're right," Stephen said.

"People could die!"

"So you said."

Stephen stepped away, but Bernard caught his arm.

"There is a man in the city who may be able to help you more than I have done," Bernard said. "Giles asked me to recommend a man who could perform a certain service. I come across such people now and then, and I gave Giles his name."

"What sort of service?"

Bernard shook his head. "I cannot say much more. I won't be a part of this. And I don't want my name connected with it."

"Who was this man, then?"

"Lambekyn le Gathard. People call him Lamb, but he's anything but a lamb. You'll find him most likely in the Red Candle on Thames Street. That's where he holds court."

"I don't know it."

"It's by Douegate in All Hallows in the Hay. Be careful around him. He's dangerous."

All Hallows in the Hay was one of London's many parishes. It lay along the waterfront, where the Douegate wharf could be found. The wharf was one of the small and narrow ones, although ocean-going ships tied up at the end of it, where the water was deep enough. The Guildhall of German Merchants lay just down Thames Street from it and Hanseatic League ships were licensed to moor here. So, even though it was a small wharf, it was busy and always clogged with vessels.

There were taverns and inns all about the wharf to serve the sailors and anyone else seeking the comfort of women for a price, ale and wine that wouldn't choke you, and a bit of gaming for money. In one spot seven in a row sat side by side on one side of the street and five in a row on the other, each with a man or woman before the door crying out the virtues of their particular establishment in a cacophonous attempt to lure in customers from those hurrying by. Now and then, one of the criers would grasp a sleeve and make the plea. Sometimes this was successful; other times it earned them a shove and a curse. But they were persistent and kept up the harangue.

The Red Candle stood out less than any of the others. In fact, it was easily missed, for it inhabited a cellar beneath a warehouse. The only thing giving away its presence was a wooden sign, with a red candle crudely painted on it, on a post by the stairs. Someone had given the sign a hard knock. It hung from the post by only a single hinge that creaked as the wind pushed it back and forth. There was no crier out front.

Gilbert paused at the top of the stairs, the steps slimy with moss and puddles of water.

"It's a risk of life and limb just to go into the place," he muttered, as a woman emerged from an alley to the right carrying a wooden bowl used to piss in. She made her way around Gilbert to a trough where in due course a tanner's boy would be along to collect the urine. A passing urchin stuck out a foot and tripped her. She fell headlong, the bowl tipping and covering the front of her dress with urine as she went down and then mud when she hit the ground. The woman shrieked and lunged for the urchin, who stood by laughing and pointing at his triumph for the admiration of passers-by. But he was as agile as a deer and leaped away, disappearing into an appreciative crowd.

Gilbert added, "Ah, life in the big city."

"I imagine it's worse coming out when you're drunk," Stephen said, just as worried about the stairs. "After you?"

"No, you first. That way if I slip, you'll cushion my fall."

"Not if I see you coming."

Despite the hazard, they reached the bottom without injury, only to be knocked backward when two large fellows threw open the door and pushed into the tight space.

Stephen rubbed a shoulder jolted by an impact with the stone wall. "Sorry to get in your way."

"You should be," one of the men said. They climbed the stairs two at a time, heedless of the treacherous footing.

"They must come here often," Gilbert said, admiring their agility.

The interior of the Red Candle was dark but for a few candles and oil lamps about; no fire; the dirt floor strewn with old rushes that had been churned to mush in many places — the whole cold, dank and cheerless. The taps were to the left, behind a bar, and there were a half dozen tables with benches. Only one of the tables was occupied by two men and a woman of about twenty or so, her brown hair falling in disarray from beneath a linen cap. The woman held a large padlock in one hand and was probing in the key portal with a strip of metal. At Stephen and Gilbert's entrance, one of the men muttered, "Away with that, Dot."

The woman dropped the lock into her lap, and took up a mug.

"Looks like someone got lost," Dot cracked.

"What'll you gentlemen have?" asked the man behind the bar who was wiping wooden mugs.

"Ale," Stephen said.

"Sure you won't have wine?" the barman asked. "I've a wonderful Bordeaux. It's just off the ship!"

"Go on!" one of the men at the table called out. "Go for the wine! It's like nectar."

"Maybe you'd like some of the Rhenish if your gullet's too soft for Bordeaux," the woman said.

"It's too early in the day for me," Stephen said.

"Oh, you are a dull boy," Dot said.

"People keep saying that," Stephen said.

The barman produced mugs of ale and handed them to Stephen and Gilbert.

"You didn't come to my fair establishment for my fine ale," said a grey-haired man with a broad jaw rimed with white stubble and muscular shoulders. "What brought you here?"

"I'm looking for someone," Stephen said.

"Why would that be?"

"I have questions. I hope he has answers."

"And who is the fellow?"

"I'm told his name is Lambekyn le Gathard."

The room fell silent. Stephen could hear the straw crinkling under his feet. The people at the table, with the exception of the grey-haired man, looked into the corners.

The grey-haired man drummed his fingers on the table that were surprisingly long and delicate to be at the end of his knotty forearms, eyes narrowed in thought.

"I'm Lamb le Gathard," he said at last.

"Pleased to meet you," Stephen said.

"I'm sure. What do you want with me?"

"I understand you're acquainted with one Father Giles de Twet, and that you met him a couple of weeks ago."

There was that crypt-like quiet again.

"Father Giles de Twet." Gathard seemed to roll the name around in his mouth as if getting a taste for it, one he did not care for if his sour expression was any guide. "Why're you asking about him?"

"He was found dead in the Thames at Windsor Bridge a few days ago. I've been asked to help in the inquiry into the cause of his death."

"By whom?"

Stephen almost said Prince Edward. But an instinct stayed his tongue. London had thrown its support behind Montfort and the rebellious barons. Only two weeks ago, the king and Edward had trapped Montfort and his closest supporters in Southwark, but Montfort escaped when the people of London threw open the bridge gates for him. People here were unlikely to help someone associated with their enemy.

"The coroner of Berkshire asked me to make inquiries while I am in the city on business. It is known that Father Giles returned from London the day before his death. There are concerns about what he was doing here before he died. Some connection, perhaps. I don't know."

"Never heard of the man."

Gathard met Stephen's gaze, but the others kept their eyes averted.

Stephen drained his mug and put it on the bar. By the emphatic way Gathard had spoken, he was sure he wasn't going to get anything more out of the man. "That's that, I suppose. Good day to you, then."

Stephen turned to the door and went up the stairs.

"You lie better than that Gathard fellow," Gilbert said when they reached the top without falling to their deaths. "I really like that bit about the coroner of Berkshire. Inspired."

"Thank you, Gilbert. Your encouragement is a balm to my flagging spirits."

"Just don't get used to it."

"I know you too well for that."

It was getting close to noon, which meant it was time to think about dinner if there was no other business taking precedence. Gilbert had said nothing about his appetite so far as they strolled up Thames Street, but Stephen noticed him sniffing at the aromas from the cook shops lining the street — scents of baked meats, roasted meats, fried meats, and the mouthwatering smell of fresh bread and pastries. Not even the competing stench of horse manure or the fresh contributions from dogs and the piss troughs along the way could overpower the beckoning delights of the cookhouses.

Stephen was not in the mood to patronize a cookhouse, however, since that meant eating in the street in the cold. He wanted a fire to warm his hands and feet in the hopes that the thaw would extend to his head, where his thoughts had frozen.

They came to a tavern near the Queenhuthe wharf that went under the sign of a Blue Heron, one spindly leg on the head of a fat man peeping from a barrel.

"What about that place?" Stephen asked. "It looks several cuts above the Red Candle."

"A tent filled with shit is a cut above the Red Candle," Gilbert said.

"Gathard would be disappointed to hear that opinion. I'm sure he takes pride in his establishment."

"I have the feeling that running a tavern isn't his main business."

"Whatever made you think so?"

"Just a feeling."

"I thought we weren't supposed to rely on those."

"I am a mere clerk. My job is to make sure you don't rely on them. It does not work the other way around."

Since Gilbert's objection to Stephen's dinner choice was not forthcoming, Stephen went in. As he hoped, there was a good fire burning and even a place by the fireplace close enough to enjoy some of the warmth. The floor was dirt, but at least it had been swept clear of rotting straw. Bundles of herbs sat in vases on each table to lend fragrance to the air. Stephen settled on a bench, feeling for drafts, a constant problem in any house, but he did not detect any. One could only hope that the quality of the food and ale was up to the surroundings.

A servant hurried over. "What will you have, my friends?"

"Ale for the both of us, and whatever is in the stew pot," Stephen said.

"What would that be, by chance?" Gilbert asked.

"It's beef with leeks, carrots, and turnips, and a good helping of beans thrown in." the servant said

"That should do nicely," Gilbert said.

"You will not be disappointed," the servant said with a grin as he went off toward the kitchen.

"I hope not, for my sake," Stephen said. "If that belly of yours is not satisfied, I'll not hear the end of it till supper." He steepled his fingers. "Now, tell me, what leads you to think that the tavern is not Gathard's sole business?"

Gilbert pulled on the corners of his mouth. "His shifty nature, for one. And the fact that that woman was practicing picking a lock, for another. You saw it, surely?"

"Hard to miss. A den of thieves, you think?"

"I would put money on it," Gilbert said. "What would Father Giles want with a band of thieves?"

"Perhaps he wanted something stolen," Stephen said.

Stephen stroked his chin as the servant returned with bowls of stew, a platter of bread and cheese, and mugs of ale.

"Let us suppose that Father Giles needed something stolen," Stephen said.

"Hard to think of what that might be," Gilbert said through a mouthful of stew.

"It is. Now, if he had access to this thing, whatever it is, he probably would have done the deed himself. But he didn't. We can speculate that it was locked up somehow."

"Somewhere in Windsor?"

"Most likely, don't you think? In a place so difficult that it needed someone with special skills to get to. Not the sort of someone you're likely to run across in Windsor."

"But in London there is no end to iniquity, and the skills to exploit it."

"Just so," Stephen said. "So, Giles consulted with Father Bernard, who, as he said, runs across such people in his line of work from time to time."

"But how would he know them?" Gilbert covered his mouth with a hand. "Oh, dear, the confessional!"

"I would think so. Don't priests in the cathedral have to take their turns hearing confessions?"

"Depends on the cathedral. It's considered a tedious chore, so often the job goes to the newest ones."

"Let us suppose, however, that Father Bernard takes a turn from time to time."

"A bit of a suppose," Gilbert said.

"Perhaps. And perhaps not. It is certainly a strong suppose Giles knew that Bernard might have met such people now and then."

"Surely, you do not suggest that good Father Bernard shared the subjects of confession!" Gilbert shook his head in disapproval.

"Very possibly," Stephen said. "Even likely. Don't priests talk shop like ordinary folk?"

"I would not put it past them, especially if a bit of wine is involved," Gilbert said glumly.

"So then, Bernard gave Giles Gathard's name. Giles hired Gathard to carry out a bit of theft."

"It is speculation built upon speculation — a castle of sand."

"Have you got any better ideas?" Stephen asked.

"No. Give me a few moments and I will no doubt come up with some."

A few seconds passed in silence.

"Do you think that two horses were part of the price?" Gilbert asked.

"Seems plausible," Stephen said mildly, savoring Gilbert's surrender but avoiding the temptation to rub it in; it was a castle of sand, after all, and he could easily be wrong. "The horses would have been necessary to get Gathard's thieves to Windsor and back. I doubt they wanted to walk. Stands to reason, they were part of the price."

"And the day after they get to Windsor, they burgled whatever it is they burgled for Giles," Gilbert said.

"Which suggests that whatever Giles wanted stolen, he knew exactly where it was and how to get at it," Stephen said.

"Do you think they had a falling out? Giles and Gathard? Perhaps the thieves didn't recover the thing Giles wanted, and he refused to pay them the rest of the price?"

"Could be," Stephen said. "Or they demanded more. I wish I could think of a way to find out. I can see now why Gathard wanted nothing to do with any talk of Father Giles. He didn't want to be implicated in the crime."

The stew was so good that Stephen and Gilbert ordered a second bowl each, along with the bread to go with them to mop the sauce, and a good hour passed in comfort by the fire.

Nothing short of snuggling under a thick blanket brought as much pleasure in the winter as a good fire and a good meal.

Toward the end of that time, Gilbert excused himself to visit the privy in the rear garden, wrapping his cloak about him in preparation for plunging into the cold.

Stephen rested his hands on his chin, savoring the glow from the fire. For the moment, he pushed away thoughts of the problem of Giles' death and what he had to do about it.

The tavern door opened, admitting a blast of cold air and six burly men. Five were dressed in the red woolen coats and red hats of London bailiffs. The clubs in their hands reinforced that impression. One of their number, however, was one of the men Stephen had seen earlier in the Red Candle. The buzz of conversation died.

They paused by the door and looked around. The man from the Red Candle pointed at Stephen and said, "That's him."

Stephen rose as the bailiffs strode toward him. This clearly meant trouble, but he could not guess why.

"How can I help you fellows?" Stephen asked.

"You're under arrest!" one of the bailiffs declared. He grasped Stephen's arm, while another bailiff grabbed the other.

"What for?" Stephen asked.

"Spying."

"That's absurd," Stephen protested. "Who says so?"

"I do!" spat the man from the Red Candle. "You offered us money to help you find out what the city plans to do to aid the barons!"

"I did no such thing!" Stephen declared.

The bailiffs jerked Stephen toward the door.

"Wait!" Stephen said. "I have to pay the bill. You don't want to stiff the keeper of this fine tavern, do you?"

The bailiffs paused. Eyebrows rose at this unexpected request.

"All right," one of them said.

"How much?" Stephen asked the servant who had brought their food.

The servant named an amount. The bailiffs let go of Stephen so he could dig into his purse. Stephen counted out the cost, which he handed to the servant.

Then he pushed the guard on his right, drove a shoulder into the one on his left, and ran for the door to the kitchen.

Gilbert heard the yelling and clamor as he reached for the latch on the rear door to the tavern.

Primal instinct made him dodge to the side, which saved him from being knocked over as the door burst open and Stephen ran out.

Stephen tossed his purse in Gilbert's direction and dashed across the yard toward the back wall, followed closely by five men in red coats and red hats.

Gilbert had no idea why five men in red coats would be in pursuit of Stephen, but he suspected they represented local authority. And not wanting to be swept up as well for whatever bad thing they imagined had occurred, he edged behind the nearby woodpile and crouched down just as a sixth man came through the door — one of the brutes he had seen in the Red Candle.

His heart pounded with fear, expecting to be found out and arrested, too. But the brute's footstep crunched on the gravel walk as he put distance between himself and the tavern.

Meanwhile, Gilbert heard the unmistakable thumps of clubs striking flesh, accompanied by shouts of "Stop resisting!" and assorted curses. He chanced a look around the woodpile. The five men were standing over something on the ground and raining blows upon it. That thing had to be Stephen: they had caught him before he could vault over the wall. As good as Stephen might be, no mortal man could take on five men at once.

Shortly, the redcoats tired of the beating and hauled Stephen to his feet. Blood ran down Stephen's forehead and there were red marks on his face that likely would turn blue with bruising after a time.

Gilbert ducked down again, hardly daring to breathe, as the redcoats dragged Stephen back into the tavern.

He waited for some time, taking deep breaths to calm himself, before he entered the kitchen at the rear of the tavern.

A cook was shoveling coals out of the fire in order to fry swan necks in a skillet.

"What was that about?" Gilbert asked the cook.

"Some spy for the royalists they've arrested," the cook said, heaping up the coals and not bothering to look around.

"Where would they have taken such a criminal, I wonder," Gilbert said.

"The city gaol, where else?" Satisfied with his pyre, the cook placed a grill with legs over the coals and put the skillet on top. He turned around to grope for some butter for the skillet.

"The city gaol," Gilbert murmured. "Of course, how silly of me. Wouldn't be the Tower, would it."

"Since the Tower's in the king's hands, that's the last place they'd go." The cook dropped a large smear of butter in the skillet and watched it melt. He frowned at Gilbert, puzzled at the questions.

Gilbert felt the stare as if the eyes were daggers. Had he been too nosy? Had he said something that gave him away?

"Well, I should be going," Gilbert said. "Is there a back way out? I've been meeting a lady friend and I don't want my wife to find out I've been here."

One side of the cook's mouth turned up. "There's a gate out back. Don't leave it open."

Gilbert lingered in the doorway of a pottery shop down the street from the Brittany Inn. He pretended to be fascinated by the painted pitchers, mugs, jars and cups covering the counter and shelves beyond it, but his real attention was on the street and the people in it. He didn't see any red-coated bailiffs, but he wasn't taking any chances. He had no idea how the bailiffs had found them in that tavern, but that they had done so raised the possibility that the bailiffs knew of their lodgings as well and were lying in wait. If that was the case, though, he had not spotted any of them, or anyone who had his eye on the inn, either. He should have been heartened by the fact that across the street from the massive inn, which stretched almost all the way from Ludgate Street to Paternoster Street, was the high wall enclosing the west side of the cathedral close. That wall made it impossible to miss anyone lingering in the street for purposes of watching the inn.

Still, he was afraid to walk in, and collect their horse, mule and belongings. What if bailiffs were waiting inside instead of in the street?

The proprietor of the shop finished with a woman customer and turned to him. "Can I show you anything?" he asked.

"Well, I, uh, I," Gilbert stammered. "I, uh, wondered if there is a back way into the inn's courtyard."

"For what purpose?" The proprietor stroked his black pointed beard.

The question was posed with a measure of hostile suspicion, but Gilbert had a lie ready. "I have a lady friend waiting for me there. Unfortunately, my wife has found out about her, and may be waiting to surprise me in the hall."

"You — with a lady friend! Well, there's no accounting for taste. You look harmless enough."

"Oh, I am quite harmless!" Gilbert exclaimed, realizing that the shopkeeper thought the lie he had offered could be a ploy for robbery.

"Come on. I'll show you the way."

The proprietor led Gilbert to the hall, where he called out, "Jane! I'll be right back! Mind the store!", and through the house to the rear garden, which backed on a narrow lane. As with all the land bordered by the city's major streets, this lane rambled about through small hovels of one and two-stories, connecting with a maze of other similar lanes. At last, they emerged between a timber structure that resembled a barn — probably a storehouse of some kind — and a shed covering a massive woodpile.

The proprietor beckoned at the open space beyond. "There you are."

"Thank you so much," Gilbert said with relief.

He expected the proprietor to turn away, but the man stuck out a hand. Gilbert stared at the hand until it struck him that the man wanted payment. Well, that was only fair. Gilbert dug into Stephen's purse and laid a farthing on the palm. The hand remained where it was. Gilbert deposited another farthing, then another and finally a fourth. This satisfied the hand, which closed around the shards of silver coin. Gilbert made a mental note to put down in his account book the expenditure of one penny for miscellaneous expenses.

"Good day to you," the proprietor said and turned back to his shop.

Gilbert remained where he was, surveying the courtyard while he planned what to do next. Obviously, barging in might not be the right thing to do. It might, for instance, startle waiting bailiffs into action. He didn't want that.

All right, then. Gilbert slipped around behind the woodpile to the stable. It was a short dash to the stable door, but he forced himself to walk quickly rather than to run, as his feet insisted he do.

Once safely inside, he listened for the sounds of someone raising the alarm, but all was quiet. This was a relief, but he wasn't out of the dark woods yet.

He saddled and tacked up Stephen's mare and his obnoxious mule, but left them in their stalls for the time being.

As he came out of the mule's stall, he bumped into one of the boy grooms.

"What you up to, sir?" the boy asked. Spotting the tacked-up horse and mule, he added, "Leaving? Or just going for a ride."

"Just going for a ride," Gilbert said, trying to sound nonchalant. "Over Southwark way. It's too long a walk for my friend. He has a bad foot, you see."

The boy nodded. He had seen Stephen limping when they came in last evening. "Right, sir. Well, if you need anything, just call out." He pointed upwards. "I'll be up there, in me chamber."

"Thanks. I will." Gilbert could not restrain a smile at the boy's reference to his attic space among the spare hay bales as a "chamber."

While the boy climbed the ladder to the attic, Gilbert again returned to examining the inn surrounding the courtyard. The inn buildings formed three sides of the yard. And they were three-stories tall, the intervals between the black-painted timbers white rather than light blue as they were facing the street. There was a porch running the length of each floor so that the doors to the chambers opened into the courtyard. Stephen and Gilbert's chamber was at the bend at the far left by a stairway.

Again, Gilbert spotted no suspicious characters in red coats, or in coats of any kind, for that matter. Well, there was nothing for it but to take the plunge.

This time, however, he remembered to put up his hood so that if anyone looked out a window in the hall to the right, he would not be easily recognizable. He thought this plan quite clever.

It was clever enough to see him safely across the yard, and before he knew it, he had climbed the stairway to the second floor. He put his key into the door lock, pushed the door open and peered in, wary of the possibility of red coats waiting inside. A pleasantly empty chamber greeted him.

In haste now, he scooped up Stephen's war gear, their satchels and saddlebags, and raced down the stairs.

It was impossible for Gilbert to refrain from running to the stable. The urge to be away was as powerful as his need to breathe.

He pulled the mule out of his stall, mounted him and took up the mare's reins.

Gilbert clicked his tongue and squeezed the mule's sides with his calves. Ordinarily, nothing happened when Gilbert did this, and it was the same now. So, he gouged his heels into the mule's sides and urged him forward with his seat. Often this had no effect as well, but today was different. The mule bolted out of the stable so abruptly that Gilbert's grip on the mare's reins nearly pulled him from the saddle, and badly strained his arm.

The mule knew a way out when he saw it, and trotted energetically toward the passage to the street. There is no worse gait than a fast trot to jolt a rider, and the mule was giving it his best, perhaps as punishment for having been heeled so hard. Gilbert bounced about and clung to the cantle of his saddle, fearing a tumble at any moment.

As the mule neared the passageway, five red-coated bailiffs emerged from the back door to the hall.

"Hey, you!" one of them shouted. "Stop in the name of the law!"

"I don't know how!" Gilbert shouted as he dug in his heels to drive the mule into a canter. Oh, Lord, how he hated cantering — only a little less than he hated trotting. But it was the only thing he could think to do.

Two bailiffs attempted to bar the passage, but dived out of the way to avoid being knocked over and trampled as the mule thundered through. One bailiff managed to secure a grip on Gilbert's left leg and the tug pulled his foot from the stirrup. He had never ridden a horse or mule without both stirrups and the fact he'd just lost one filled Gilbert with terror. Yet he kicked his trapped foot free and kept going, fumbling unsuccessfully for the lost stirrup.

The mule reached the street and, without any instruction from Gilbert, turned sharply left. Gilbert almost kept going straight, which would have flung him into the wall of the cathedral close, but by some unknown saint's intercession, he remained in the saddle.

He could not get the mule to slow down until they had entered Paternoster Street.

Chapter 8

The mule had turned right at the corner instead of left, and so had taken Gilbert deeper into the city.

Once the mule tired of running, Gilbert was able to recover the lost stirrup. This gave him the confidence to check the mule and the mare for whether they had lost any of their possessions. Everything seemed to be there.

The short winter day was ending, the sun about to sink behind the tops of the houses, so Gilbert gave some thought about shelter for the night. The prudent thing would be to get out of the city where angry bailiffs had no authority, and yet he could not leave. He had to do something about Stephen, although he had no idea what. Something would occur to him, though; he was sure of it. The unfortunate thing about that was, it would be dangerous, and possibly life-threatening. As much as he enjoyed Stephen's company, a thing he could never admit out loud, of course, for some reason it always involved a high risk of death and great discomfort.

He reached the end of the cathedral close, where Paternoster Street emptied into the broad expanse of Westchep, the location of the greatest of the London markets. There were inns aplenty along here, and he had enough coin to afford a bed for the night even if most of it wasn't his and was supposed to be spent on things that benefited Lord Geoffrey de Geneville. But because of the fact that an innkeeper would be forced to provide his name, even if it was a false one, to the ward alderman, he felt compelled to think of another plan. Being an inherently thrifty man in all things as long as it did not involve books, another idea occurred to him.

He turned down a lane that ran south along the east side of the cathedral close. London was full of lanes that wandered about and often dead-ended (or so it had seemed behind the Brittany Inn), but this one ran relatively straight, so Gilbert followed it in hopes it found Thames Street.

Shortly, the lane dead-ended where a big parish church occupied one corner of the intersection. The mouth of another street opened a brief distance away to the right. That one probably met Thames Street. But now that Gilbert was nearer Thames Street, he began having second and third thoughts about whether to take it. It would be easier to find his intended destination if he did, but Gathard's men and the city's bailiffs might find him more easily there, a prospect that filled him with dread.

The cross street, however, was one of those west-east thoroughfares, so on impulse Gilbert decided to take that one. From the piles of rotting fish here and there and a litter of scales, the street looked like it held a fish market.

At the corner where the fish market ended, Gilbert glanced down the street to the right, wondering if he dared cut down to Thames Street — and stopped dead.

About fifty yards off, where the street bent to the left just beyond a church, was Maggie's brothel.

He urged the mule to turn down the street, but he refused to move.

Gilbert dismounted, and pulled him by the bridle. The mule resisted at first, tossed his head and tried to bite him, but Gilbert persisted and eventually the miserable beast gave way and followed him.

There were iron rings attached to the side of the brothel for tying off horses. Gilbert did so, but advanced no further into the house than the threshold because he was fearful of someone carrying off his and Stephen's possessions, not to mention the animals themselves.

Gilbert opened the door and called, "Is Mistress Maggie here?"

A woman who was short and fat and not a whore poked her head out a doorway on the other side of the entrance hall.

"What do you want with her?" the woman demanded.

"A word."

"What, are you a bill collector?" she demanded suspiciously. Then recognition dawned. "Oh, it's you. One of the fellows who came with Ida."

"Yes, indeed, that would be me," Gilbert said, wondering if he should be glad or alarmed at being recognized. Recognition often made you feel warm inside, but today the prospect rendered his innards rather chill. "The small, unimportant one."

"Don't just stand there in the doorway," the fat woman said. "You're letting in the cold. Have you no idea what wood costs these days?" She drew Gilbert in by the sleeve.

"Er, no," Gilbert said. He resisted being drawn in but the fat woman was rather strong.

"Well, it costs quite a lot. Now, wait here," she said. She slammed the door shut, shot him a disapproving look for his ignorance, and lumbered up the stairs to the first floor.

Presently, Maggie came down. "Ah, Master Wistwode. Come for some refreshment and diversion?"

"Well, no," Gilbert said. "I, uh, need a place to stay the night."

Maggie's mouth turned down. "We are not an inn. You know that."

"Yes. But I'm rather reluctant to patronize one, you see. We've had a spot of trouble with a gang of fellows on Thames Street. They've kidnapped Sir Stephen and are after me, too, I'm afraid. They think there's a ransom in it. They've sent men around the inns of the city asking after me."

Maggie snorted. "You're not worth two farthings, but I imagine they'd think Sir Stephen is worth rather more."

"Will you help? Give me a place to hide for a day or two?"

Maggie looked put out. But she said, "I suppose. But it will cost you."

"What do you mean Stephen's been kidnapped?" Ida demanded as she strode across the hall from the kitchen in the rear of the house.

Gilbert wrung his hands together. "I'm afraid it's true. We need to talk."

Gilbert told her the story on the way to and from a stable in Fish Street, where the fish market took place, to put up the horses.

Ida hugged her cloak about her shoulders against the cold as Gilbert finished while they stood in the twilight outside the Church of Saint Nicholas Olave across a lane from the brothel. But it wasn't the cold of the evening but the cold of her heart she sought protection from.

"He's in the city gaol?" she asked.

"As I said, that's what I was led to believe."

"By a cook in a tavern. And you believed him?"

"I don't see any reason why not to. Where else would city bailiffs take a prisoner?"

Ida paced back and forth before the church door. "We will have to be certain. Where is this gaol?"

"I don't know."

Ida shot him a hard look that plainly said he should have done more. "We'll have to find it, then. Maggie or one of the girls will know where it is."

"Can you ask without giving away our interest?"

"Leave that to me," Ida said grimly. The dimple on her chin appeared as she pressed her lips together.

"And if we find him there?"

"Then we'll have to find a way to get him out."

Chapter 9

The sun had barely risen before Ida and Gilbert were on their way.

They stopped at a cookhouse in Fish Street, where Ida bought a fresh loaf of good rye bread still hot from the oven and some dried apples. At a butcher shop a bit further on, she bought a large sausage that the butcher bragged had been seasoned with pepper. She verified the claim about the pepper by smelling the sausage, since the stuff was rare and costly; the assertions of merchants could not always be trusted. All of it went into a basket, covered with a cloth.

Ida's informant had told her the main city gaol lay at Newgate, and that seemed most likely where Stephen had been taken. But when she and Gilbert presented themselves at Newgate, one of the wardens informed them he had no Stephen Attebrook as a prisoner.

"You could try Ludgate," the warden said, hooking a thumb toward the west. "But that's for crown prisoners. You say your fellow is charged with being a royalist spy?"

"That is the accusation," Ida said.

"Then I'd look for him at one of the sheriff's prisons. There's one beside the guildhall, which is not far from Crepelgate. It's closer, so I'd try that one first."

"I don't know London," Ida said. "I have no idea where the guildhall might be."

"It's not hard to find," the warden said with the air of a man who was often asked to give directions; London was a sprawling and confusing place and outsiders easily got lost. "Take Wodestreet. It's on the left just after Saint Peter's. Keep going. You can't miss it."

This seemed simple enough, but Ida and Gilbert reached the north wall at the end of Wodestreet without seeing anything that looked like a guildhall. An inquiry of a skinner, who was working in front of his house to remove the skin of a fox, sent them back the way they came, and advised them to be on the lookout for a tavern under the sign of a golden boar; turn left there and follow the lane through to the end.

The Corpse at Windsor Bridge

When they reached the end of the lane, there was no mistaking the guildhall. A garden lay before it planted with apple and cherry trees. The building itself was large, square and tall, whitewashed and clean, with a red-tiled roof.

The gaol was behind the guildhall at the edge of a yard. From the front, it looked like any other house. What distinguished it was behind the house stretched walls nine feet high.

Not knowing what else to do, Gilbert knocked on the door to the house.

A stout woman with thick forearms covered in flour answered the door. Gilbert stepped back, removed his hat and said politely, "Good day to you, mistress. Lady Ida here," he indicated Ida with her basket, "wishes to see one of the prisoners. She has brought him sustenance."

"Lady Ida, is it?" the woman said, eyes narrowing taking in Ida's gown, which was the same one she wore when she rode away from Windsor. "And who would this prisoner be?"

"Sir Stephen Attebrook."

"Why does she want to see him?"

"She is his niece. And as I said, she's brought sustenance. To lighten the burden, you may have to feed him."

The woman "hmphed!" and said, "Wait here."

She shut the door.

After a time, the door opened again. A stooped man with hollow cheeks covered with grey stubble looked down upon them.

"You want to see one of our guests, eh?" the stooped man said.

"Yes, sir, if that wouldn't be too much trouble," Gilbert said.

"It's always trouble." The gaoler's lips worked and one hand clutched the edge of the door as if he was considering slamming it in their faces. Then he eyed the basket, which was emitting pleasant odors of fresh bread. He licked his lips. "Well, I suppose I can spare a moment."

The gaoler held out his hand.

"How much for your trouble?" Gilbert asked hastily, taking the hint.

"A penny will do," the gaoler said.

Ida almost protested. A penny was a full day's wage for an ordinary man and so was quite a lot of money. But she held her tongue.

Gilbert surrendered the penny, and the gaoler came down the steps followed by a large man with a squashed nose who carried a club. The gaoler and his companion led them around the side of the house, where a door pierced the wall. The gaoler unlocked the lock securing it and led them into a confined space.

"What is this place?" Ida asked.

"Ah, it's the exercise yard," the gaoler said. "Now I'll have a look in that basket."

Ida did not want to give it over, but the gaoler's hand, held out to her, beckoned insistently.

The gaoler flung the linen towel into the dirt and peered into the basket, avarice in his eyes. He broke the loaf in half, probed within each half with a finger, then put one of the halves under his arm and returned the remaining one to the basket. Ida seethed.

The gaoler did not stop there. He cut up the sausage into bits and kept half of it, too. He bit off a fragment of sausage and chewed with an open mouth, revealing a wide expanse of gums that hardly seemed up to the task. Yet somehow, he managed it.

"This is quite good," the gaoler said with a grin. "Will you be coming again?" He tossed a hunk of sausage to the man with the club, who ate it without comment.

"Tomorrow," Ida said, suppressing the urge to hit the gaoler over the head with the basket.

"Ah, I would be pleased if you brought some more of this excellent sausage."

"If the butcher still has it, I will be pleased to," she said.

"Thank you," the gaoler said. "Now, this way."

He stepped to another door in the far wall across from the one through which they had entered. This one was also locked, and after a bit of fumbling, during which the gaoler dropped the half loaf and several pieces of sausage, he finally got the door open.

Beyond the door was another enclosed space, though smaller than the exercise yard. There were two doors to the right and two to the left, which Ida guessed opened into cells where the prisoners were kept, since faces could be seen peering through the bars of the windows in each door. It was a drab and horrible place that looked full of pain. The stench of human waste was overpowering and so foul that she wanted to mask her face with the hem of her cloak.

"Stay here," the gaoler said while the man with the club positioned himself in front of the entrance way.

The gaoler unlocked the far door on the right. "Attebrook!" he shouted into the darkness within, "you've a visitor! All the rest of you! Remain where you are!"

Stephen stumbled out into the wan December light. Ida suppressed a gasp at his appearance. He had a big cut on his forehead that had scabbed over, but the tracks the blood it had let out still streaked his face and there were large spots of it on his coat. His forehead held bruises as well, as did his cheeks. His upper lip was split on the left side.

"Hello, Ida," Stephen said. "You really shouldn't have come."

"I brought you something to eat," Ida said. "I thought you might be hungry. You have such an abominable appetite." She raised the basket.

The gaoler waved her forward.

"That is good of you," Stephen said, examining the contents, which he then removed.

"I hope you still have enough teeth left to enjoy it," Ida said.

The man with the cudgel laughed.

"All there, although a couple are loose," Stephen grinned.

"Don't bite down too hard, then, if you don't want them to fall out," Ida said.

"I'll be careful."

"I'll be back tomorrow," Ida said. "Should we find you a lawyer?"

"I think that would be a good idea," Stephen said.

"Enough!" the gaoler commanded. "Back in your cell!"

Stephen eyed the man with the cudgel as if measuring whether he could take him. But he made no such attempt.

"Tomorrow, then, Ida," he said.

She nodded, and said to the gaoler, "Shall we go?"

"Are you sure about this?" Gilbert asked, voice heavy with concern.

They were across Thames Street from the entrance to the Red Candle. They had been here for some time while Ida worked up her nerve to go in. Several men had come and gone, all striding quickly like men going about their business rather than men seeking a simple mug of wine or ale in the afternoon. However, the street was crowded with traffic, so they did not stand out and no one had paid Ida or Gilbert any mind.

Ida's heart pounded as if it was a wild bird beating its wings to escape the cage of her chest and fly away. She felt faint, nauseous and sweaty. The fact was, she was terrified. She couldn't force herself to take even a single step toward those stone stairs leading into the earth. She thought about the kind of men in there, hard, violent men who would not hesitate a wink about harshly using a young girl like her. And she knew well how that was. She had lived a sheltered life until six months ago hard, violent men had kidnapped her and sold her to be a slave, used by a pitiless lord as an object for his pleasure, a vessel for his brutal passion.

Until Stephen had come for her.

"It has to be done, doesn't it?" she said.

"I could go," Gilbert offered for the tenth time.

Ida put on a face which she hoped made her look stern and determined, although she was grateful for Gilbert's willingness to protect her, but he could not do that now and he knew it. "They'll remember you. They'll give you nothing but a beating and turn you over to the bailiffs. You know that."

Gilbert nodded bleakly.

"It's too dangerous," Gilbert said. "There has to be another way."

"Do you know of any place that has what we need?"

"No." Gilbert shook his head.

"And neither did Maggie. It has to be the Red Candle, or nothing. And Stephen rots in gaol. People die in gaols, you know. Especially in winter."

She smoothed the folds of the plain, brown gown she had changed back into at the brothel with its soiled apron so as not to look out of place on the street. A linen wrap covered her blonde hair and a worn linen cap sat on top of that so that she seemed much like any common young woman in the city. Or she hoped so.

"You better get out of sight," Ida said.

She took a deep breath, fingered the dagger she carried in a pocket of the gown, and started across the street.

Ida had never been in a tavern before; young ladies of her station rarely frequented such places, even in Ludlow. Her only experience with public houses was the Broken Shield Inn, which was sedate and genteel as such places went. So, the interior of the Red Candle came as a shock. It stank of rot; the straw underfoot, so far as she could see it in the light of the two oil lamps illuminating the place, was churned up to mush and decomposing. The tables looked knocked together by someone who needed lessons in carpentry, and they were battered and worn. Someone had tipped over one of the benches and no one had bothered to set it upright.

There were two men at a table on the other side of the chamber, hunched over mugs, their faces bright from the light of the lamp in the center of the table. They were big hard men, with stony faces, and they looked Ida over with the same expression a cat regarded a mouse it had trapped in a corner. Ida took several deep breaths hoping this would slow down her heart; it did not have any noticeable effect.

The prospect of stepping in the rotting straw was more repulsive than having to step into ankle deep mud; at least mud washed off with water, while the rot could permeate the leather and might be impossible to get out.

Nevertheless, she couldn't just remain in the doorway. She shut the door and advanced across the chamber to the two men at the table.

One of them rose to face her.

"Well, what's a little girl like you doing here?" he asked. "You got something to sell?"

Ida thought he believed her to be a whore. She shook her head. "No, I'm looking for Dot. Is she here?"

"Dot? What you want with Dot?"

The man who had spoken advanced on her. Ida gave ground until her back struck the bar separating the taps from the rest of the house. The man put his arm on the bar beside Ida and leaned close. His breath smelled of sour ale, onion and tooth rot. Close up, she saw he was over forty; his nose was lined with spidery red and blue veins.

"I need to talk to her," Ida said, as firmly and calmly as she could manage. Don't show fear, a voice said in her head. That will make things worse.

"You a friend of hers?" The man said this as though he did not believe it was true.

"I have business with her," Ida said.

His head and that foul-smelling mouth drew closer. He smiled, maliciously, like a predator, the smile reshaping into the beginning of a kiss.

Last summer, after Ida had been kidnapped by slavers, Stephen taught her how to use a dagger. *As much as you may depend on others for protection, you know better than anyone that the time may come when they aren't there and you have to rely on yourself*, he had said *Left foot forward, left hand up before you. Dagger at your right hip. Don't extend the weapon until you mean to stab the man. Otherwise, he may take it from you. And when you attack, commit yourself fully to it. Drive the blade home without reservation, twice to the body and then once overhand to the neck*. The other thing he had said, which had made her want to recoil with horror, was, *Keep stabbing until he goes down.*

These thoughts ran through her mind as she drew the dagger from her pocket and put her left hand on the man's chest. She didn't want to stab him, but if he didn't back up, she would do it.

As the brute pressed closer, she shoved him as hard as she could with her free hand. It felt as though she was shoving at a post, but to her astonishment, the man lurched a half step backward.

The man saw the dagger at Ida's right hip, her left hand before her. For a moment, Ida thought she would have to act, that he would not believe she was serious or that she might be a threat.

But he withdrew his hand, took one step back and regarded Ida appraisingly. He clearly had seen people stand with knives like this and understood what it meant and what his chances were even if she was a mere woman and slender as a sapling. *A smaller person can defeat a larger one if he is determined enough*, Stephen had said. *And having a knife makes a big difference.*

"Business, eh?" the man said. "You'll find her in the back garden, taking her ease. So to speak."

He backed to the table and sat down.

The other man pointed toward a door at the rear. "You can get there that way."

Ida edged to the door and glanced inside. It was a storeroom jammed with sacks, boxes and barrels that smelled musty and thick with dust, but there did not seem to be anyone lurking within to leap out in ambush as she passed through. A stairway climbed to a back door at the rear of the storeroom.

Still, there was the possibility the men in the tavern might follow and attempt to overpower her. She slammed the door and ran to the stairs, heart pumping at the thought the back door might be locked and she would be trapped.

To her great relief, the back door opened, and she climbed to the garden, glad to be out of the fetid cave that was the tavern.

There was no one in the back garden. Ida even checked behind the woodpile, which towered higher than her head. As she came back around it, however, there was a woman holding up her skirts and marching from the direction of the privy.

"Are you Dot?" Ida asked.

"I could be," Dot said. She gave Ida the up-and-down, assessing the clean and generally well-tailored gown Maggie had procured: it marked her as someone with a bit of money, though not a lot. "Why?"

"I need your help."

Dot scoffed. "Help you? How?"

"I need to learn how to pick locks."

"You want to know how to pick locks, eh?" Dot asked.

They had taken seats on a grey bench that swayed a bit as they sat down, but fortunately did not collapse. Ida was grateful for the bench, even as she doubted it would hold up, because its availability meant she didn't have to go back into the tavern and face the stench and the stares of those men.

"Whatever for?" Dot continued, with amusement.

On close inspection, Ida saw that Dot was a rather pretty girl with full, rosy cheeks and a small agile mouth. Dot was only a few years older than Ida, too, no more than nineteen or twenty. But she already had lines about her eyes from care and perhaps too much of an affection for wine.

Ida looked down at her hands folded in her lap. "I need to get in a certain room."

"What's in the room that is so important to you that you need to break in?"

"There are things there."

"What sort of things?"

"Things that can be sold."

"And why would you want to sell these things?"

"To pay my brother's fine."

"What's happened with your brother?"

"He's being held in Oxenford gaol. If I don't find a way to pay his fine, they'll cut off his hand."

"Why would they do that?"

"He's accused of poaching. But he didn't do it!"

"Of course, not." Dot looked thoughtfully toward the Thames. "You know, if this room is rich enough, there might be those who would take on the work for you. For a fee, of course."

"Really?" Ida asked.

"Hereabout the Red Candle there are those who specialize in such things, getting into locked houses, strong rooms, and the like. They are available for hire."

"That's so hard to believe."

Dot chuckled. "Why a couple of people here, whom I cannot name of course, just burgled a place for a client — but a few weeks ago."

"Why ever would they do that?"

"The client, a stinking rich cleric, said his property was in hold there. He was willing to pay a huge amount to get it back. It was too easy and well-paying a job to pass up."

Ida held her breath for a couple of heartbeats, and then asked as disinterestedly as she could, "What could be so dear to him the he would risk so much?"

"A gold cross with jewels," Dot said. "On a gold chain."

"So he just paid up and you went on your way?" Ida asked with what she hoped was disbelief leavened with disinterest.

"That's the size of it. We are professionals, after all. Now, about your problem."

"It's very dangerous."

"How so?"

"The room of which I speak is in Wallingford Castle, a strong room in the tower," Ida said. She had never been to Wallingford Castle, but it wasn't more than a day's ride from London. She knew of it because she had heard one of Percival FitzAllan's sergeants, who had been in the garrison there, talk about it. "It's well guarded. Surely you'd get caught."

"Hmm. And you can get to it?"

"I am a servant there. No one pays attention to what I do or where I go."

Dot was quiet for a moment, hands on her knees. "It's going to cost you."

"I did not expect you to work for free." Ida removed the ruby ring from her pouch. "Will this be sufficient?"

She had considered using some of Gilbert's money. But a girl like she was pretending to be wouldn't have any. But a ring? That could be explained . . . .

Dot took the ring and gazed at it with undisguised surprise and avarice. "Is this real gold?"

"Yes."

"And the stone, what is it?"

"A ruby."

"Where did you get it?"

"From the locked room."

Dot chuckled. "And there's more where it came from, eh?"

"Yes."

Dot put the ring in her pouch. "All right then. What kind of lock is on the door?"

"I'm not sure."

"Girl! Locks are different. Each one must be handled differently, according to its nature."

"Oh." Panic began to overwhelm Ida. She had not thought of this.

"Tell me what it looked like. Was it a padlock?" Dot asked.

"No," Ida said. "It was one of those attached straight to the door."

"Ah," Dot said. She produced a square iron lock from beneath her cloak. "Like this?"

"Yes."

"A warded lock, then. You don't need to pick a warded lock. You only need a skeleton key."

"What's that?"

Dot produced a key ring with five keys on it. Each of the keys had a round stem. At the end of each stem were sets of small metal protuberances, not unlike sets of wings; two with just a pair opposite each other, two with two pairs and one with three.

"It's easy enough to do," Dot said. She made sure the lock was secure. Then she inserted one of the keys, jiggled it a bit, and the lock opened. She handed the lock and set of keys to Ida. "You give it a go."

Ida accepted the lock, made sure it was fast, and inserted the same key Dot had used. She jiggled the key as she'd seen Dot do. The lock did not come free, and she began to worry that there was more to it than Dot let on.

But then there was a soft clunk, and the lock disengaged.

"Look at you," Dot beamed. "Almost a professional already."

A strange city, particularly one as large and maze-like as London, was not a place where either Ida or Gilbert wanted to wander about in the dark, even if it was Christmas Night. Not only was there the possibility of getting lost, but there was the chance of robbery, or being accosted by the roving bands of bailiffs which patrolled the streets during the night despite the holiday.

So, they found a small tavern in which to settle down late in the day and await the arrival of nightfall. The tavern was packed to the brim with people celebrating, and it was impossible to get to the privy out back without pushing people aside or knocking them over.

The crowd had hardly thinned even three hours after sundown.

Gilbert touched Ida's hand. "I think we should go. We've given the gaoler enough time to get thoroughly drunk, don't you think?"

"I hope so," Ida said standing up.

They made their way to the door, where a boy was letting out lamps for those stepping into the night. A person carrying such a lamp was considered to be on lawful business after dark and so was unlikely to be arrested.

"Should we take one?" Ida asked Gilbert.

"Yes, I think so," he said patting the rope wound around his ample belly. "Let's not take any more chances than we have to."

"Right, then," Ida said, paying the boy a farthing while Gilbert carried the lantern.

The street outside was named Aldermannebury, they had learned, and they walked north along it, savoring the chill air. A light dusting of snow was falling, which worried Ida. If it remained on the ground, there might be trouble. But the snow appeared to melt upon contact with the ground, although it stayed on the rooftops, looking like someone had flung fresh flour over them.

They reached the lane leading to the guildhall and began to pass people coming from its direction, while others hurried by them toward the hall.

The guildhall itself was lit up, lights in every window. There was a noisy crowd out front clustered around a bonfire. The door to the hall opened, revealing blazing fires and another crowd within.

"Perhaps we should try another night," Gilbert said. "When it's quieter."

"No," Ida said grimly. "Everyone will be drunk, as you said. And their noise will cover ours."

"I hope you're right," Gilbert said with trepidation.

They found the gaoler's house dark and quiet.

"Good," Ida said. "They're either passed out or gone to the guildhall."

They crept around the side of the gaol.

"Here, I think," Ida said. "Let's have the rope."

"Oh, dear," Gilbert muttered.

He unwound the rope, then tied it about his chest under the armpits.

Ida tied the other end to her belt.

"Give me your hands," she said.

Gilbert made a stirrup of his hands. Ida put a foot in the stirrup and climbed to Gilbert's shoulders. Even though she was a small girl who didn't weigh very much, Gilbert grunted and grimaced at the weight.

Ida had thought she should be able reach the top of the wall, but it remained several inches away from her outstretched hand.

"You'll have to push me up," she hissed.

"I'm not sure I can," Gilbert said. Nor was he steady on his feet; he wobbled and trembled, and there was the real possibility that he might fall over, which could make a lot of noise and ruin everything.

"Mind your head, then," Ida said.

Before Gilbert could protest, she stepped on the top of his head, and gained a handhold on the top of the wall. She wasn't strong enough to chin herself, but she managed to pull herself high enough to throw a heel to the top of the wall. With three limbs working rather than a mere two, and assisted by Gilbert's efforts raising her other leg, she was able to pull herself up. She rested a moment while straddling the wall, and untied the rope from her belt. She dropped the end into the open space within the gaol where the cells were located. She was so afraid now that her limbs seemed made of water that would not obey the commands she gave them.

"Get ready," she whispered. "I'm going over."

Gilbert nodded, still not fully recovered from the insult to his head, and grasped the rope with both hands.

Ida let herself down into the yard. Above the cells on the left was an upper floor to the gaoler's house, which had two windows. She paused and listened for any movement, or any sign from those windows if anyone was there and heard anything. But only the muffled sounds of merriment from the guildhall reached her ears.

Ida tip-toed to the door to Stephen's cell. She put her lips to the barred window. "Stephen, are you there?"

The sounds of rustling issued through the little window.

"Ida, what the devil are you doing here?" Stephen hissed from the dark, for she could not see his face, although she felt his warm breath. He sounded shocked and surprised. Ida was strangely pleased with that.

"I've come to fetch you home," she said.

"What are you going to do? Break down the door?"

"Of course not, silly man. Just wait a minute while I work a little magic."

This came out more confidently than she felt. She fished in her pouch for the skeleton keys, fumbling for one of them. She wasn't even sure if any of them would work and her hands trembled as she directed the first key into the keyhole. The key rattled in the hole, but did not budge the lock. She tried a second one. Similar result. She tried a third. Still no joy. But on the fourth, after some struggle, the lock clanged and the door opened.

Stephen slipped out into the yard. "Where'd you learn to do that?" he asked, amazed.

"That's a secret," Ida said.

Then eight other men pushed through the door.

"Who are they?" Ida whispered.

"My cellmates," Stephen said. "We can't just leave them behind."

Then a voice came clear as day from another cell across the yard.

"You'd better let us out, too. I'll shout if you don't! I'll call the gaoler!"

"You'd better work fast," Stephen whispered to Ida.

The others already free saw the rope and the first of them began to climb to the top.

"I don't like this, Stephen," Ida said as she applied her key to the lock. "We should be away. Every moment we lose may mean our capture."

"I know. But I don't think we have a choice."

Fortunately, the same key Ida had used on the lock to Stephen's cell worked on all the others, and she had them each unlocked with only a moment of fidgeting. Soon, the yard was crowded with men; how many Ida had no idea. Those cells must have been packed wall-to-wall.

The men were sensible enough, however, not to make excessive noise while they waited for their turn to climb the wall. And one by one, they went up and over. In their haste, some of them didn't bother with the rope; a pair of men boosted up another, who slipped over and disappeared.

Ida watched the windows in the house overhead as she waited her turn. Now that her work was done, she wanted nothing more than to be away, hidden by the dark night.

"That is an idea," Stephen murmured, watching those ascending without the rope. "Up you go, Ida."

He put his back to the wall as Gilbert had done and boosted her onto his shoulders. Grasping her ankles, he lifted her even farther so that she easily grasped the top and got a leg over. Then she hung from the other side, and dropped.

In moments, Stephen was at her side.

"How did you do that?" she gasped. "Fly?"

"Almost," Stephen grinned. "It's really a rather short wall. Easy enough to jump. Get out of that thing, Gilbert. We must be off."

Gilbert wormed his way out of the rope and handed it to the man beside him. "Your turn to be the anchor," he said.

"But you did so well," said the man offered the rope. He flung it down and raced away.

"What now?" Gilbert asked Stephen.

"We've done what we can," Stephen said. "It's every man for himself now."

As they came around the corner of the gaol to the south side, they heard a cry of pain from the front, followed by a squelching sound and then another.

"We better run," Stephen said, taking off at the limping lope that passed as a run for him.

Ida gathered her skirts and easily kept up with him; she felt as though she could leave him behind if it was a race.

"Hey!" a voice shouted. "You! Stop!"

"Shit," Stephen spat. "It's Matt."

"Matt?" Ida asked.

"The gaoler's bully. As mean as they come."

They glanced back and in the gleam from the guildhall saw Matt, his cudgel in his hand, running full out toward them. He was shockingly fast for such a large man.

There was a chance that Stephen and Ida might have outrun him, even with Stephen's bad foot, but there was no chance that Gilbert could get away.

And Matt was rapidly closely on him.

"Damn it," Stephen said as he skidded to a halt.

He turned back.

"Stephen!" Ida cried. "What are you doing?"

Stephen passed a stumbling Gilbert and ran straight toward Matt. Matt slowed and raised his climb to strike Stephen down, certain of the success of his intention, his mouth a rictus of cruel joy.

But Stephen ducked left as Matt's mighty blow descended so that it hissed by Stephen's head.

Stephen drove the Y of his hand against Matt's throat and threw him on his back with such force that Matt's feet flew into the air and his head struck the ground with an audible thonk. Matt did not move.

"Serves you right, you vicious bastard," Stephen said turning back to Gilbert and Ida.

They ran into the dark side by side.

Chapter 10

The sun hardly had time to rise above the rooftops before word of the great Christmas gaol break had spread throughout the city. Early morning visitors in need of relief, some still nursing hangovers from the festivities of the holiday, brought news of it to Maggie's house, and then people on the streets could be heard discussing events loudly under the windows, so that all the girls, and Maggie herself, were agog over it. Much hilarity was enjoyed at the expense of the gaoler and the aldermen who had hired him.

Meanwhile, the rumors darted about: the gaoler had been sacked; the gaoler had been made a guest in his own establishment; the gaoler's helper had been killed; the gaoler's helper hadn't been killed but instead badly mauled by escapees; there were more than forty escapees, some of them murderers, arsonists and rapists, now free to prey upon the innocent and unsuspecting.

People were warned to keep a lookout for the most notorious criminals, including a royalist spy who had recently been arrested before he could do any harm to the barons' cause, as well as the beautiful young woman who had visited him the day before and was seen helping him escape. It was said that the militia had been called out to scour the streets, and double guards had been placed on the city gates to recapture the fugitives should any decide to flee the city.

The part about the militia appeared to be true. Stephen observed two men carrying bills walking up and down Bred Street in front of the brothel, accosting passers-by. If this was true, he believed the rumors about the gates being guarded as well.

Then later in the morning, the ward alderman's men came round and interrogated Maggie about whether she had entertained any suspicious guests.

She went to Gilbert's chamber, where Stephen was hiding, after the interrogation.

"You can't stay," she said to Stephen, Gilbert and Ida. "None of you. The girls are in danger of being questioned.

Any one of them could let slip that I have been harboring illegal guests. I cannot risk it. I want you gone as soon as possible."

Stephen poured out another shilling from his rapidly depleting purse, and gave it to Maggie. "For your trouble, Maggie. And thanks."

Maggie smiled faintly. "I always had a soft spot for you. A foolish thing, but there it is."

"We'll be gone by noon," Stephen said.

"See that you do," Maggie said.

They were out of the house a full hour before noon.

They went out the back to avoid being noticed. Stephen led them through a maze of lanes bordered by huts, decaying tenements and lots filled with rubbish, where goats and chickens wandered in the ruts, a large pig challenged a pair of dogs over fresh scraps, and even a rabbit escaped from a hutch was seen fleeing behind an overturned cart lacking wheels, and washing hung on lines so thickly overhead that in some places it obscured the sky and dripped showers on passers-by.

They reached a larger street and turned south toward the river.

At Thames Street, they said good-bye to Gilbert, who rode away on the mule, towing the mare. The plan was that he would cross the river to Southwark at London Bridge and meet them on the other side. Stephen and Ida would cross by ferry since they were likely to be identified at one of the city gates, while the riverbank stretched for several miles and was harder to patrol.

The tide was starting to go out when they reached the river.

"Welcome to Brokenwharfe," Stephen said.

"Why do they call it that?" Ida asked as they found a seat on the ground above the high tide line, where a dozen people were waiting about a fire.

The Corpse at Windsor Bridge

Stephen pointed to a line of pilings at the tide line that leaned this way and that, like a set of bad teeth. "They've never been able to keep them up. They keep falling down."

Everything about London seemed both marvelous and frighteningly strange to Ida, and the riverfront, which she had never seen before, was no exception. The receding tide exposed broad mudflats that on close inspection were a prairie of rubbish: bits of lumber, the remains of sunken boats, and such. Gangs of small boys were prowling about with sacks, salvaging things from the mud. Occasionally, when a boy found something he would announce his discovery with a whoop. A fight broke out over one such discovery between rival gangs who pummeled each other with their fists, gobs of mud and what had to be stones, for the latter missiles drew blood from one boy. The victors scampered up to the shore, bearing their prize.

Ida was delighted to see the river filled with ships and boats, since she had heard that London was the busiest port in England. The big ships mostly were moored to posts in the river, and only one of them was moving, a cog being towed by two rowboats through the drawbridge in the middle of London Bridge about five-hundred yards downstream.

The bridge itself was a marvel of whitewashed stone and blazingly white and black timber houses rearing high upon a span that seemed impossibly far from shore to shore. She could see people moving over the bridge in the gaps and many waiting for a drawbridge in the center of the span to lower and allow them passage.

She noticed that Stephen kept scanning the river, watching the many rowboats going up and down and to and fro. He was growing restless and she wondered if that was because none of the boats seemed to be coming here.

"Are we in the wrong place?" she asked.

Stephen glanced at the people around the fire. "They aren't waiting for fish to jump out of the river to them. There should be a boat along soon."

Stephen's head began to nod. His eyes closed and he leaned back against a post. "Wake me when a boat comes."

Ida took this order seriously, since she was anxious to get away. Despite the fascination the city held for her; she would have enjoyed it more if she was safe, but she felt like a fly about to be swatted.

Nonetheless, she found herself struggling to stay awake. She had not got much sleep because of the terror of the gaol break and the flight through the city. Fatigue caught up with her now. She swore that she would fight against it; that she would close her eyes for just a moment to rest them . . . .

Ida awoke sometime later. She sat up, appalled that she had fallen asleep. She looked about. The sun was lower, and the mudflats had grown in expanse. The people about the fire were gone, and the fire had burned down to almost nothing.

But a boat was putting into shore almost directly in front of her, a single oarsman struggling with the oars.

Ida shook Stephen. "Wake up. Our boat is here."

"Oh, what?" Stephen said groggily, rubbing his face. He looked unusually pale, which made the black stubble of his beard and his eyebrows stand out all the more, the bruises on his face and the scab on his forehead as well.

Ida held out a hand and helped Stephen to his feet.

They started toward the boat, which had grounded on the mudflats, waving and calling to the boatman.

"You there!" a voice shouted from their right. "Hold!"

Ida's heart leapt at the sound. She glanced for the source of the voice — six men altogether — and felt Stephen grip her arm hard.

"Keep going," he said. "Pretend you didn't hear them."

"Is it the watch?" Ida asked, frightened.

"Yes."

They stumbled through the mud toward the boat, the muck clutching at their feet, making progress slow.

"You there!" the voice repeated. "I said stop! We must have a look at you!"

"A look at you!" Ida gasped. "What does he mean?"

Stephen touched the scab on his forehead. "Perhaps they're looking for a man who's had his head broken open." He gave her a push. "Run!"

Ida ran through the muck as well as she could, which is to say there was a lot of stumbling involved, but fortunately, no falling down.

She looked back just before she reached the boat to see Stephen some distance behind her, but with three men on his heels.

"You, the boat!" one of the more distant watchmen shouted. "Remain there if you want to keep your license!"

The ferryman waved, indicated that he intended to obey.

Ida reached the boat and clutched the saxboard, her chest heaving.

"Can you not away?" she cried to the ferryman.

"And lose my license?" the ferryman said. "Not a chance."

Ida heaved with all her might against the side of the boat. It stuck in the mud for a moment, but since there was only a single man in it, she managed to push the boat far enough that it floated.

She climbed into the boat and drew her dagger. She pointed it at the ferryman and said, "Get ready to start rowing."

"Not a chance." The ferryman crossed his arms.

"You pretend that I'm threatening your life and you do it," Ida panted. "And when we get across, we'll give you enough money for a dozen passengers."

The ferryman considered this proposition for a blink of an eye. He put his hands on the oars and shouted, "She means to kill me! Help!"

Ida dared to look back and saw three of the watch catch up with Stephen. He halted, stepped aside and clouted one of the watchmen on the head. The man fell into the mud. A second watchman swung a club at Stephen's head, which he parried with an outstretched arm and then drove a fist into the man's mouth; that one went over backward, landing with a splash. The third watchman swung crosswise at Stephen's body. He tried stepping back to avoid the blow, but the mud caught his feet and he fell on his back. The watchman raised the club two-handed to strike a great downward blow. Stephen kicked him in the groin. The watchman doubled over as Stephen got to his feet and stumbled the last few steps into the river, where he flung his satchel into the boat and clutched the side as it bobbed away from shore.

"Now, row, for your life depends on it," Ida snarled as menacingly as she could, dismayed at her voice's squeaking quality. Murderer's voices should be low and growly, not so high-pitched as hers. She shook the knife at the ferryman for emphasis to make up for it.

The ferryman's mouth twitched as if he was about to laugh. But he shouted "Don't kill me! Please don't kill me!"

He dug the oars into the river for a mighty stroke.

"Southwark, if you please, my good man," Ida said, settling on a thwart.

"Of course," the ferryman grunted with the strain of a stroke. "My pleasure."

"At least the river got some of that mud off," Ida said as Stephen crawled dripping over the saxboard.

"Do you have any idea how filthy the Thames is?" he asked, narrow eyed. He brushed off a turd that had found a perch on a shoulder.

"No, but I do now."

Chapter 11

The innkeeper at the Abbot of Waverly's Inn in Southwark refused to allow Stephen inside until he had stripped off his filthy clothes and washed thoroughly. Although people were inured to stinky smells, there were limits, especially in confined spaces and around food.

The shedding of clothes was easy enough, although it meant standing naked in the cold; at least he was in a barn and not in the yard in full view of anyone at the inn who cared to watch. Washing could be torture in any weather, for often one had only cold water and a cloth. However, the innkeeper provided tepid water lightly heated over the cooking fires, which reduced the torment.

Stephen left his filthy clothes in a pile and dipped a washcloth in the basin he'd been provided. He hastily washed himself, the gritty lye soap abrading his skin.

Ida entered the barn while he was working toward his ankles.

Stephen dodged behind a post, which did not do much to conceal his nakedness.

"Not done yet?" Ida asked, turning her back. "Hurry or you'll miss supper."

"Ah, yes," Stephen said, edging from behind his post. "Thanks."

He finished with the washcloth and toweled off, shivering and teeth chattering.

Ida giggled at the chatter. "I never heard such noise! It's a miracle you don't break a tooth!"

"M-m-my teeth are tough enough," Stephen said. He pulled on his spare shirt and his braises.

Ida saw this out of the corner of her eye. Since the shirt fell halfway to Stephen's knees, she was spared being inflicted with a view of Stephen's private parts. She watched him retrieve his spare stockings and lift a foot to put them on.

This caused her to turn about and push Stephen onto a nearby stool. "Idiot, your feet are still filthy."

Stephen glanced down at his feet, particularly the left one, which was missing from the arch forward. He glanced at Ida for her reaction, expecting revulsion, because she'd never seen it before. She didn't seem to notice.

Ida dipped the washcloth in the basin, squeezed it out, and handed it to Stephen. "Do you know what to do?"

"I think I can figure it out." Stephen washed one foot, and drew on the stocking for that leg. He washed the other foot and finished with the stocking, followed by his boots

"Now that's better," Ida said, hands on her hips. "Warm now?"

"Not yet," he said.

"Let's get you inside, where there's a fire," Ida said.

She picked up his filthy clothes, which she held at arm's length. She carried them into the yard where she dumped them into an iron cauldron with other clothes.

"Did it hurt much, when you lost your foot?" Ida asked as they reached the inn's door.

"I didn't feel a thing at the time," Stephen said.

"So, you're going to rule out the boys at the Red Candle," Gilbert said as a servant cleared away the debris of their supper: goose in a mushroom and mint sauce, with a hint of mustard.

"A moment," Gilbert said to the servant before Stephen could reply, hastening to dip bread in the remaining sauce on the wooden trencher. "This is quite good, you know. I shall have to consult the cook for the recipe. Our guests will like it. And Edith will be glad I brought back something other than bruises and saddle sores."

"I am glad to see that the fare is up to your high standards," Stephen grumbled, staring into the fire blazing in a fireplace so large that two men could have lain down in it head to foot and not touched the sides. The fire put out a delicious warmth so that he was beginning to recover from his bath. "We never want to disappoint."

"And yet so often you do," Gilbert sighed. "Whenever we take our journeys," he added for Ida's benefit, "our sad lot is nothing but suffering, sleeping in damp fields, and inferior food. Edith seems to think that we have such fun on these outings. She is so wrong."

"I don't think she really wants to know what you get up to," Ida said. "Breaking people out of gaols! You are such a man of danger, Gilbert."

"Hush, hush," Gilbert said, alarmed. "Someone might overhear! It is the talk of the city, after all."

"About the Red Candle," Ida said, taking up the thread Gilbert had cast down. "What do you think, Stephen? Are they your killers?"

"You said that they had stolen this cross, Giles paid them, and their business was done," Stephen said.

"That's what Dot said." Ida wiped her small mouth with her napkin and laid it on the table, where a servant scooped it up with her vacant trencher.

"We don't even know for certain that this client of theirs was, in fact, Giles," Gilbert said.

"Maybe you want to go back to nail down this detail, although I am satisfied with the mention of a stolen cross," Stephen said.

"There is that," Gilbert said "But if the client *was* Giles, Dot would never confess they killed him after a falling out. And falling out with thieves is rather a common thing." He leaned over toward Ida. "I keep no company with thieves, so it's only what I've heard."

"Of course," Ida said, sipping her wine. "And I'm sure you'll tell me if it's common for thieves, in such falling outs, to kill their clients."

"Those who don't pay," Gilbert said, with the air of a well-informed man. "What if they saw this cross — which was a fabulous work, I tell you, as I saw it with my own eyes, who's to say they didn't up their price? And when Giles refused to meet it —" he drew a finger across his throat, then realizing this was wrong, under the circumstances, added, "Splash!"

"That's just it," Stephen said. "Dropping a man into a river with a rock tied to his feet isn't a London thief's usual style of murder. Nor is leaving behind all the gold he had on him."

"Ah, you are an expert on London thieves?" Gilbert murmured. He spoke aside to Ida again: "He spent a dissolute youth here, you know."

"I heard him confess to that very thing," she said.

"Did you really?" Gilbert sounded surprised. "Oh, yes, he did, didn't he. I had forgotten."

"And my mother spoke of it," Ida said.

"How could she have heard? Hafton, after all, is far from London," Gilbert said.

"She has friends at Westminster," Ida said. "Stephen was often in trouble and embarrassing his master, Ademar de Valence — insolence, getting into fights, gambling in the city, consorting with women of ill repute, that sort of thing. Or so we heard."

"And we have seen he is on very good terms with brothel keepers," Gilbert muttered. "You know, Lady Ida, I wonder if it is a good thing for your reputation to remain in his house! You might be fatally compromised!"

"I shall have to take my chances," Ida said.

"It's common sense," Stephen said, ignoring these remarks about his history, which unfortunately were true, and trying to draw the conversation back to the people at the Red Candle. "Why would they resort to something so elaborate? Not to mention difficult to pull off without anybody noticing. A knife in the gut is straightforward and so much easier. London thieves are skilled but they lack imagination and flare."

Gilbert shrugged in what Stephen took to be a general indication of agreement.

"That means we have to inquire further in Windsor," Gilbert said. "Although I doubt it will do much good. That field's been well ploughed by others."

"We will have to plough it again," Stephen said. "One good ploughing and perhaps we can give up and go home."

"A little poorer than when we got here," Gilbert lamented. "The finder business is not very profitable I'm afraid, my lady."

"So I am finding out," Ida said. "Although you seem to live rather well while doing it." She glanced around the inn, which was well fitted out, with dark wood paneling and even wooden floors, so rare at inns. "Unlike where I was made to spend my evenings."

"The only problem that remains," Stephen said to Ida, "is what to do with you."

"If you are thinking that I should find refuge in another brothel, you are mistaken," Ida said. "I've had enough of brothels. Too much racket in the evenings to get any sleep. And one of the clients thought I was a working girl. It took two of the others to pry him off me. Disgusting man."

"You didn't want to use that handy dagger of yours?" Stephen asked.

"It could have made a mess," Ida said. "And no doubt would have provoked all sorts of questions."

"You shouldn't go back to Windsor," Stephen said. "FitzAllan's still there and his men might see you."

"They won't be looking for a common girl," she said, waving her hand at her simple gown. "Who would look twice at this?"

"Any young man?" Gilbert said softly.

Ida went on as if he had not spoken, "We can find lodgings for me in some out of the way place, and I will keep my head down. When you are done with this business, we can go home."

"Just home," Stephen said. "To Ludlow."

"Yes," Ida said.

"You weren't safe in Ludlow before."

"Perhaps things will be different this time," Ida said.
"She's either optimistic or sorely addled," Gilbert said.
"I'm leaning toward addled," Stephen said.

Chapter 12

It was almost sundown when they reached the southern edge of Windsor town on the road from Stanes. A cold wind carrying the scent of rain blew steadily across the road, creating tiny waves in the puddles from the recent snowfall that had melted.

Stephen was glad to get here at last, and he was sure the others felt the same. Ida shivered with each gust of the wind.

He had given a great deal of thought on the road from Southwark about what to do with her once they reached Windsor. He had to find a place where she could remain out of sight until he and Gilbert finished their business here, which he had decided to do straightaway. That is, it was more important to get Ida away from here than to find Giles' killer. So, he would spend a day making further fruitless inquiries, and then declare to Prince Edward that he had been unable to discover anything. With that, he and the others could vanish into the west country and hopefully be forgotten.

He examined the houses in southern Windsor as they plodded by. Most of them were peasant holdings here at the extremity of Morstreet, surrounded by substantial yards with gardens and a few empty lots between them.

A short distance before Morstreet struck Sheetstreet at a fork, there were two inns across the street from each other. The sign on the one on the left was of a red rooster and the one on the right was of a green man pouring the contents of a keg into a wooden mug.

They dismounted outside the Red Rooster. Gilbert went into the Green Man to ask about rooms while Stephen went into the Red Rooster. Ida held the horses.

Stephen and Gilbert met a short time later in the street.

"Nothing there?" Stephen ask at the concerned expression on Gilbert's rosy face.

"No," Gilbert said. "And you?"

"No luck. The proprietor said that the town was full up because of the king's presence."

"But we got a chamber at that place up there." Gilbert hooked a thumb toward the marketplace. "The Golden Swan."

"Maybe we got lucky," Stephen said. "Anyway, he recommended the house of a friend of his in Underore."

"Where's Underore?" Gilbert asked.

"Behind that chapel where we examined the body," Stephen said. "The friend lets out space in the barn."

"I don't fancy sleeping in barns," Gilbert grumbled. "I've never found a barn convivial." He glanced at Ida as if for her support. It was scandalous for a gentlewoman to sleep in a barn.

"I don't mind a barn," Ida said. "It will be a new experience."

"You won't sing the same tune after one night in it," Gilbert said.

"You'll find that I complain less than you do," Ida said.

"I'm not complaining," Gilbert protested.

"Of course, you are." She smiled, patted his arm, and they walked up the hill toward the castle.

Stephen and Gilbert walked up to the barbican the next morning shortly after sunup. A castle at that time of day was just waking up with hardly anyone about, but such was not the case today.

The lower bailey was a scene of much rushing to-and-fro and confusion: wagons and carts being loaded, laden carts and wagons being brought down from the middle bailey, horses being saddled, servants and soldiers hurrying here and there amid a great deal of shouting. It had all the hallmarks of the impending departure of a great personage. Then Stephen remembered that the king and prince were set to leave for France and a confrontation with Simon de Montfort to be mediated by King Louis.

Someone mistaking Stephen for a sergeant of the retinue shouted in his face, "What the devil happened to you? Fall down a flight of stairs? Quit standing around with your thumb up your arse! Get packed and make sure your horse is ready!"

There was nothing to say to this but to nod and stammer, for the officer who had done the shouting was in no mood for anything else.

When the officer passed on to his next victim, Stephen and Gilbert edged around the throng and hurried up the slope to the gate to the middle bailey, where they had to wait for some time for a long line of wagons and carts to get through.

More carts and wagons were coming around the ditch encircling the great motte from the upper bailey, and there was another long wait to get through the last gate.

A crowd of well-dressed magnates had gathered outside the queen's chamber. Stephen recognized FitzAllan in the crowd in a heated discussion with the king himself. King Henry seemed to be listening thoughtfully to what FitzAllan was saying, nodding now and then. But when FitzAllan paused for breath, the king's slender hand made a chopping motion and FitzAllan's mouth drew down at the corners.

"It will have to wait until we get back," the king said, his voice penetrating a gap in the hubbub. "I'm sorry, but I just don't have the time to deal with such a little thing right now. The girl holds only a single manor, after all, and even that is in dispute. And the matter of her possession will have to be decided first. If she's not the heir, then the crown is not interested in her."

"What about the prince?" FitzAllan asked. "Can he be authorized to hear the matter in your stead?"

The king looked thoughtful again, as if he was seriously considering this proposal. Then he shook his head. "Small as this thing is, it requires action by the crown, not by a deputy. Prerogatives, man! You understand this, surely."

FitzAllan drew a breath. "Of course, my lord."

"It won't be long before you have satisfaction," the king said. "We'll be back within a month. I shall hear the case personally then, even though as you can see, I am very busy."

"Certainly, my lord," FitzAllan said bowing.

"Good," the king said.

Then he strode toward the gate to the middle and lower baileys. Most of the crowd followed him, including FitzAllan.

This would bring them close to where Stephen and Gilbert were standing. There was nowhere to hide, apart from the stone stairway leading up the motte to the squat tower on top, so Stephen drew Gilbert through its doorway.

Stephen caught a glimpse of FitzAllan in conversation with Prince Edward, and heard Edward say, "I'll be staying a few more days after all," then they were gone.

He peeked out of the doorway and saw Edward's wife, Princess Leonor. She was resplendently dressed, regal-looking from her broad, flat hat, snow white silk vale falling down her shoulders and back, and a flowing blue-and-white striped overgown. There was something about the overgown, though: it was belted about her middle with golden cord, but just below her breasts — higher than normal, for it should be about the waist. A gust of wind revealed why. The breeze drove the overgown hard against her abdomen, which was unreasonably round and protruding for such a slender woman, like a man's misplaced pot belly.

Stephen realized what that mound meant. She was pregnant; only by four or five months, he guessed, remembering how his wife Taresa had looked at that time. The recollection of her sparked a pang of grief mixed with guilt: he had not thought about Taresa in months.

Isabel preceded the princess into the queen's hall.

Stephen's plan had been to seek out Winnefrith and ask him about the cross. But the sight of Isabel changed his mind.

Leonor was by a large blazing fireplace, her feet up on a stool and a blanket covering her legs. A servant was handing her a mug of something hot and steaming. Stephen had seen her only once before, on the morning of Giles' funeral, and her appearance, as tired as she was, was arresting. Without trying, she dominated the chamber, slate-colored eyes that turned in his direction as he came toward her, narrowing with a question, the delicate lips compressing, the narrow chin rising up and the thin nostrils flaring as she took a breath, her expression at once concerned and a bit apprehensive? While he expected her to take offense at being approached by someone as lowly as he, her face relaxed with a slight smile. The hands upon her abdomen remained where they were and made no move to signal dismissal either to him or to the servants who surrounded her.

Isabel occupied a chair at her side. She saw Stephen, leaned over and said something to Leonor.

In contrast to Leonor, Isabel's face was hostile.

Stephen stopped.

The princess nodded and beckoned Stephen to come closer.

He came forward and bowed.

He was about to say his name when Leonor interrupted. "So, you are the finder I have heard about," she said in Castilian rather than French. "I hear you have been off to London, or some such thing."

"Yes, my lady," Stephen said.

"And you think that something happened in London that is connected with dear Father Giles' death?"

"I think there may have been, my lady."

"What on earth could it have been?"

"I'd rather not say until I know more."

"I see." She stared into the fire. "But you have come here with a purpose that has to do with Giles' death."

"I would like a few moments with Lady Isabel, my lady."

Leonor glanced up at Isabel, who nodded.

"Very well," Leonor said.

"It might be best if we could talk somewhere it is unlikely that anyone can overhear," Stephen said.

"Certainly. Isabel, kindly show Sir Stephen the chapel."

The chapel was as dim as it had been when Stephen waited there for Ida. A single open window admitted feeble light. It smelled musty, perhaps from tapestries on the walls of biblical scenes, which he had not noticed before.

Moments passed without either of them speaking. Then, Isabel broke the silence.

"Whatever do you want?" Isabel asked.

Stephen stared at her dark figure and did not answer this question. He marveled again at how a woman who could be described as plain but was in fact strikingly beautiful. He saw only half her face, one portion dressed in light from the window and the other in dark shadow. This trick of light made her chiseled cheeks stand in relief and her mouth appear as if hewn from granite, the whole accentuated by her manner, which was poised and cool. She seemed like a fencer at the beginning of a contest, alert, ready, yet he felt she was not as unfazed as she wanted him to think.

"Where is your husband, Isabel?"

"What sort of question is that? Why do you want to know?"

"I do not have to tell you why. Where is he?"

Isabel shrugged. "He is the constable of Berkhamstead Castle. I don't see what that has to do with anything."

Berkhamstead — Stephen had heard of it. It was a royal castle held by the king's brother, Richard earl of Cornwall, twenty-five miles or so away, a day's ride. Not that far. Her husband could have made a lightning journey here, done some bad business and got away easily.

"I have not seen him for six months," Isabel continued. She paced to the open window and turned, her face all in shadow now. "Our duties often keep us apart."

Her face now obscured by the dark, Stephen was deprived of the best means he had of telling whether she was being truthful. Had Isabel done this deliberately? He regretted allowing this to be the venue of their interview. He should have insisted on another place.

Stephen let the silence rule again for a moment. It was an invitation for her to fill it with more information. But she did not accept it.

"I am interested in the cross," he said. "The one you took away. What was it to Giles?"

Isabel did not answer right away. Stephen heard her breathing, slowly and with measure, controlled, yet giving the impression that she was in the grip of a powerful emotion kept in check.

"I gave it to him," she said at last.

"Why?"

"Because I wanted him to have it."

"An expensive gift."

"It was."

"Someone stole it from him, you know."

"No, I didn't," she said. She turned slightly, giving Stephen her profile, and then turned back. "Who did it? Those who killed him?"

"That seems to be the case."

"Do you have any idea who that is?"

"Not yet. Let us return to the subject of the cross. Someone stole such an expensive gift, such a *personal* gift, and he didn't tell you? That's hard to believe."

"We weren't speaking at the end."

"The end of what?"

More troubled breathing. Stephen wished he could see her face. He stepped up to her and to the side so that half Isabel's face was in the light again.

"You will not share what I say with anyone?" Isabel asked.

"If it's a confession of murder, that I cannot keep that secret. Something else, though?" He shrugged for effect. Stephen thought the answer was clear even before Isabel went on. But he had to hear it from her. It could not be his conjecture.

"It is a highly personal matter. My reputation is at stake." Her chest heaved as she breathed deeply. She said: "Giles and I — we were having an affair. I ... broke it off," she hastened to add.

"And how did he take it?"

"He was … hurt."

"For someone so interested in her reputation, why have an affair?"

Isabel sighed. "Giles was a handsome man, charming, witty, well-educated. He came from a wealthy family. I was weak. I am often alone here, and he made me feel less so."

"Why did you break it off?"

"Because it was hopeless, really. Nothing good could come of it. Do you think me a fool?"

"I am not here to judge you. Only to find out the truth, such as it is."

"I am afraid that I cannot help much with that."

"Apparently not," Stephen said. "Ah, there is one more thing. Does your husband know about this affair?"

"No. We were most discrete."

"You're sure? Keeping secrets in a noble household is very hard. The servants know everything that goes on."

Isabel put slender fingers to her temples. "Believe me. No one knew."

"How was this possible?"

She dropped her hands and glared. "You would make me share that? Details of our intimacy?"

"I would."

Her nostrils flared. "There is a confessional booth right over there." She pointed to the far end of the chapel. "It is over large to accommodate the king and queen. We met there when no one else was about. No one questions a woman going alone to church."

"At least it wasn't the sally port tunnel," Stephen said. "That's another popular spot."

"At least it was not that!" Isabel spat. "Now, if you will excuse me?"

Chapter 13

Gilbert waited for Stephen in the hall, where he lingered in a corner trying not to draw attention to himself.

"Anything?" Gilbert asked as they huddled in the corner.

"She confessed to having an affair with Giles," Stephen said.

Gilbert nodded. He had expected this revelation as well. He said, "Did she say anything about the cross, and who might have taken it?"

"She claimed not to know anything." Stephen briefly recounted the main points of the interview.

"How did she seem?"

"Cold. Detached. Not much affected by Giles' death. Insulted by questions about the affair."

"Even though she claims to be the one who broke it off, I'd have expected a bit more," Gilbert said, rubbing his chin. He looked toward Princess Leonor, who was absorbed in a conversation with a well-dressed matron, as Isabel settled onto the chair beside her. Isabel returned Gilbert's stare and he looked away.

She turned her eyes to Stephen, who held her gaze until she dropped her eyes and whispered something to Leonor.

"A formidable woman," Gilbert said, his eyes on the wall behind Stephen.

"Indeed. She's holding something back," Stephen said. "I can feel it. But there's no telling what it is short of torture. And even then, I'm not sure it would work."

"If I had to pick a woman capable of murder, she would be one of them," Gilbert said. "What if Giles found another lover? Would she have killed him out of spite and jealousy?"

"But women usually aren't capable of throwing strapping men off bridges."

"No, but they can hire someone to do it for them."

"That's true. And she doesn't look short of money." Stephen rubbed his temples. "None of this is making any sense."

"Where do we stumble off to now?"

"To find Winnefrith. There are things I should have asked him but did not. And new things besides."

Winnefrith, however, was not there. One of the valets informed Stephen that Winnefrith had left Windsor; he wasn't sure where Winnefrith had gone. But the prince's chamberlain was sure to know.

It took some time to find the prince's chamberlain, the official in charge of his household staff, because the man had gone down to the lower bailey to see the king off on his journey to France.

When they finally met, the chamberlain, a tall, lean man with thinning brown hair, who looked down his nose at Stephen and asked, "And what, sir, is your interest?"

"I am Stephen Attebrook. The prince asked me to look into the matter of Father Giles' death."

"Oh, yes. I am Edmund Viel, at your service, sir." Viel coughed. "As to Winnefrith, we really had no position here for him with Father Giles gone. So, he was sent to one of Lady Isabel's manors, where it was thought he could be of service."

"And that would be, where?"

"Ottesdun."

"And where might I find Ottesdun?"

"Just north of Oxenford about eight or nine miles or so."

"Another ride in the country?" Gilbert asked without enthusiasm as they walked down to the gate in the lower bailey.

"At some point," Stephen said. "If we really must turn over that stone again."

"Are there other, more immediate, stones to turn over closer by?"

"I was thinking of the Golden Swan. Hasn't it struck you as odd that Giles knew where the cross was hidden? It's as if he knew the thief. Yet for some reason, he was unwilling to accuse him, and instead sought to steal it back."

"You would think this thief would be long gone. I certainly would be in his shoes."

"Perhaps so. But you have the fortitude of a snail, and likely a good bit more sense. But perhaps we can find out with whom Giles was consorting in the days before his death. One of those people has to be our culprit. I am willing to guess that it was someone at the Golden Swan."

"You sound altogether too intent on solving this murder. I thought we were just going to poke about a bit and nip off home."

"We have to poke about in a believable manner if we are to be convincing to the prince."

"I just hope we don't find ourselves poking another bees' nest. For some reason that always seems to happen."

Gilbert's offhand comment about poking bees' nests rattled around in Stephen's head as they walked through the marketplace toward the Golden Swan. The market was choked with soldiers standing about among carts that should have set off with the king but had not, evidently waiting orders what to do. Barging in the Swan and asking questions of anyone in reach about Father Giles and who he might have been associating with was a sure way to ensure that such people, who undoubtedly had something to hide, would vanish into the forests surrounding Windsor, never to be seen or heard of in these parts again. Thus, some subtle and clever plan for worming out what he wanted to know was needed. The only problem was, he could not think of such a subtle and clever plan. He worried about this all the way to the door to the inn.

"You're blocking the way," a voice said behind Stephen.

Stephen turned. It was Gilbert de Clare, the young earl he had encountered a few days ago. "Sorry, my lord," he said, moving out of the way.

De Clare did not move at first, as if he expected Stephen to open the door for him. Stephen noticed that de Clare was alone. It was odd for a man of his standing to go about alone. Usually, earls and such were surrounded by a retinue of knights and squires ready to do everything for him, including wiping the shit off his ass in the privy.

Seeing that Stephen did not intend to help with the door, de Clare coughed and showed the world that he knew how to open doors without assistance.

Instead of plowing on in, however, de Clare stopped in the doorway.

"Would you care for a drink?" de Clare asked.

Stephen's mouth opened with astonishment. He had never been invited to drinks with an earl. It was an offer that could not be refused, of course, unless he felt like insulting de Clare. "Certainly, my lord."

"Come on, then." De Clare turned away.

Inn halls ordinarily were not busy in the middle of the morning, but this day was an exception. It was jammed with soldiers who had taken the opportunity, since they had not yet been ordered to take to the road, to find solace in the arms of the whores on duty and in a rapid succession of pitchers and mugs of wine and ale that were being brought from the pantry in the rear by an army of struggling servants. All in all, it was a sad testament to the officers who had lost control of the men. But this sort of thing was not uncommon where loose women and drink could be had and leadership was soft. No doubt someone in authority would be along shortly to fetch them and put a stop to the fun.

De Clare didn't have to fight to catch a servant's eye because one rushed forward as soon as he sat down, and placed a pitcher of wine and cups on the table without asking de Clare's preference. Apparently, he was well enough known that the servants knew what he liked.

De Clare filled the cups and shoved one of them across the table to Stephen.

"So, how was London?" de Clare asked. He took a deep draught and wiped a dribble off his chin.

"Busy, dirty," Stephen said. "As it usually is. Why?" He sipped from his cup, surprised that the wine was sweet; a white rather than the usual chalky red Gascon vintages to be found in most taverns and inns in England.

De Clare shrugged. "You know, we heard a strange thing the other day. From one our correspondents in London. Some of the city's men arrested a royal spy. Apparently, he was snooping around Thames Street trying to build support for the king's cause. Do you know anything about that?"

"Why would I?"

"Well, the fellow's name was given as Attebroke. Very close to your name. And neither are very common. And they could easily be confused."

"Wasn't me," Stephen said.

"And you got those marks on your face falling off your horse, no doubt." De Clare finished his cup and poured another for himself. He sounded disappointed. "You're not a spy? Edward didn't send you to London on some secret mission?" De Clare cocked an eyebrow in disbelief.

So, this was the reason for the offer of a drink. Not a bid for manly companionship but an attempt to pump Stephen for secrets that the prince had not shared with de Clare.

"I am afraid not," Stephen said. "He doesn't have that much regard for me. Certainly not for something as delicate as a secret mission."

De Clare's mouth turned down. "Well, there are few Edward thinks highly of, so don't count yourself out. And so, you know nothing about a gaol break, then. Pity, I was hoping to hear about how it was managed."

"I wouldn't know. I don't know anything about breaking out of gaols."

De Clare snorted. He leaned forward. "You broke out Bishop's Castle gaol, and Hereford Castle. And one other place I misremember. One of FitzAllan's retainers held it. No matter. London can't have been so much of a challenge for you. Unless it was Newgate. Was it Newgate?"

Stephen ignored the question about Newgate. He said, "You know about Bishop's Castle and Hereford?" It should not be surprising that word of these exploits had circulated about. Yet Stephen hadn't considered that people might think gaolbreaking was a skill he had mastered. In fact, at Bishop's Castle and Hereford, Margaret de Thottenham had made his escapes possible. He had merely taken advantage of her help, just as he had Ida's.

"Christ's blood, man, FitzAllan is still livid about Hereford and that other place you escaped from. I cannot for the life of me remember its name. Somewhere near Clun, I think it was."

"You are thinking of Bucknell, I believe," Stephen said. A year ago almost at this time, a girl had been found dead under the snow outside Saint Laurence's Church in Ludlow. To identify her killer, Stephen had traveled into FitzAllan's lands about Clun and ultimately to Bucknell, a FitzAllan dependency, where the girl's killer, her husband, had held Stephen prisoner.

"Ah, that's it!" De Clare slapped the table. "And then there's this matter of your niece. She just up and disappeared the same night as you. Tongues are wagging over that one. Where did you stash her? London, I suppose?"

"I haven't stashed her anywhere."

"Denying all involvement, eh? No one will believe you. Especially not FitzAllan. You won't keep your skin long when his boys get their hands on you, if that's your attitude."

Stephen sipped from his cup and did not reply. He knew that FitzAllan would be enraged and that, somehow, he would seek to punish Stephen. He didn't like thinking about it, nor talking about it, however.

De Clare went on. "You know, with your experience with gaols, you'll be much in demand in the coming days. People would pay well to get their family members out of hold. Cheaper than the ransoms that'll be demanded when they're taken prisoner. I would expect that breaking into a place is easier than breaking out of one."

De Clare waved a hand at the taps behind the bar where Johnnie, the proprietor, was filling a pitcher. "Look at this place. Just two weeks ago, somebody robbed the strong room. It's supposed to be impregnable, as such things go."

Stephen's senses suddenly tingled. "A robbery?"

"Oh, well, a break-in really. Someone picked the lock to the strong room and cleaned it out pretty thoroughly. Caused a scandal. The value of what was taken came to at least a hundred pounds. You haven't heard about it."

"No. This is the first I've heard of it."

De Clare shrugged. "It's not important, really. Merchants' losses. Unless you're thinking about storing something there now."

"When, exactly, did this break-in occur?"

De Clare frowned in thought. "I don't know. Let me see … You know, it was the night that idiot Giles disappeared." A light dawned in de Clare's eyes, which he fixed on Stephen. "Could he have been involved? Is that why he disappeared?"

Before Stephen could respond, de Clare rushed on, "No, that's not credible. He came from a good family and didn't want for money. And he just didn't seem the sort. Mild-mannered, bookish, given to reading poetry, singing songs and other such rot. Soft as a boiled turnip. Not the sort of man to go robbing inns."

The news that the Golden Swan had been burgled the night Giles vanished ignited a fire under Stephen and he could barely keep still with the shock and excitement of the revelation. He tried nonchalance with a dose of indifference to hide his feelings.

"You're expecting war, then?" Stephen asked to change the subject. "I thought we were trying to avoid it."

De Clare snorted, but looked pleased to be consulted about his opinion of such a weighty matter. "You don't think that this next round of talks with Montfort will make our problems go away, do you? The prince certainly doesn't. He's preparing for battle as we sit here."

"I thought he was going to the meeting in France, following the king in hopes of making peace."

"Oh, he'll be going, all right, in a few days' time. And as for making peace! That's a good one. You don't know much about diplomacy, do you?"

"I am a poor country knight. What could I know about things like that?"

"It's all about positioning, making it seem to the world, and especially the Pope, that Montfort is the cause of the troubles. Once we've made our side seem eminently reasonable and the other side recalcitrant and unreasonable, then the action will begin." His eyes narrowed. "But where will we strike, eh? That's the question everyone wants to know. Edward keeps those plans close. He doesn't share them with many people."

"Not even you, my lord?"

"Not even me," de Clare said with some bitterness and a frown, indicating that he was not as trusted and in the know as he felt he should be.

Fortunately for de Clare's disposition, the pretty blonde woman Stephen had seen him with before, elegantly dressed for a whore, reached the table. She extended a slender hand to de Clare. "My lord, I didn't realize you were here!"

De Clare took the proffered hand and smiled, the bitterness swept away. "Adeline! It lifts my heart to see you!"

"Come upstairs, my lord, and I'll lift more than that, if you please."

De Clare rose and Adeline drew him away.

But she winked at Stephen over her shoulder.

Gilbert Wistwode slipped into the place de Clare had occupied. He peered into de Clare's cup and then into the pitcher, which he sniffed.

"I say," he said. "There's still wine left."

"Go ahead." Stephen waved at him. "De Clare paid for it. You might as well enjoy it."

"What did he want?" Gilbert asked as he poured wine into de Clare's cup. "Not to be friends, surely."

"No. He thought the prince dispatched me to London to drum up support for the king."

"So he knows about the arrest," Gilbert said.

"Yes."

"Even the gaol part?" Gilbert asked alarmed, his cup pausing a few inches from his lips.

"Seems so. Although the informant got my name wrong, so there is room to sow doubt. Don't worry, you're not connected with it." Stephen refilled his cup. It was early to be drinking wine and his head was starting to float above his shoulders. "He did say one thing of interest."

"Oh?"

"The night Giles disappeared, someone burgled the strong room here."

"I say, that is interesting. So whoever stole the cross put it in hold here, you think?"

"That would be my guess, and I'm going with it. Whoever burgled the strong room cleaned it out pretty thoroughly, too, according to de Clare."

"Taking on a bit of freelance in addition to serving the client, eh?"

"Nothing like a little enterprise."

"Do you think our thief might still be here?" Gilbert said, letting his eyes wander about the hall."

"Not the one who burgled the strong room, no."

"I meant the fellow who filched the cross."

"I have no reason to think so, yet I have a feeling he still is."

"Ah, feelings. So supportive of conclusions."

"You don't think so?"

"I don't know what to think, frankly. Yet I have the same feeling, unaccountably."

Stephen down his cup and swore not to take another drop, a resolution he promptly violated as Gilbert filled his cup to the brim.

"Let us think this through," Stephen said.

"Oh, dear Lord! That will hurt so! Are you sure you wouldn't rather rely on feelings? So much less work."

"I am afraid we will have to do the work." Stephen put down his cup, having drained it by half. He was feeling warm and reckless. Perhaps he should resort to wine in the mornings more often. It did wonders for your self-regard and sense of invincibility.

He went on, "We found the cross under Giles' habit. We know it was a gift from Isabel, which he did not want to wear openly. So, whoever stole the cross needed to get under his habit."

"That is brilliant."

"Thank you. So, what sort of person is likely to get under a priest's habit?"

"The laundress?"

"Besides her."

"His valet?"

"That is not helpful."

"A whore?"

"I should think so. Is it not unlike some men to drown their disappointment at rejection in the arms of another woman?"

"Sympathy is not usually a stock in trade for whores."

"The more polished ones will cater to every need."

"You have more experience in that than I, as we have well seen. I am a happily married man."

"And I am glad you are."

An officer entered and began shouting for all of the soldiers to get outside and line up: their fun was over. Two of that officer's companions climbed the stairs to flush out those enjoying the comforts of the establishment's whores in the chambers above. Stephen hoped they were lucky enough not to disturb de Clare's revels, but from the sound of angry shouting, it seemed one of them blundered into the wrong chamber and was getting his arse chewed out over it.

It was not long before the inn had cleared out so that Stephen and Gilbert were the only ones to enjoy what remained of de Clare's pitcher in the unnatural silence, except for two broad-shouldered fellows occupying a table in a far corner.

The whores drifted over to the men in the corner, apart from the red-haired girl, Jennet, who came off the stairway and headed toward Stephen.

"Jennet!" one of the men barked. "Let those fellows be!"

Jennet halted and jerked around. "But why?"

"You girls get upstairs and get some rest. There will be a lot of work later, and you'll need all your strength."

Jennet shrugged and went back of upstairs, with the other girls.

The broad-shouldered men rose. Like several of the girls, they were dressed as a well-off merchant might be: blue and brown coats of fine material, well-fitting and newish, stockings of bright colors showing little wear and no mending, thick cloaks of good green wool. They went out to the street.

Stephen and Gilbert had finished the wine. Stephen stood up to go but his head swirled and he sat down.

"You are drunk," Gilbert said, not attempting to rise. "And on duty, too."

"I am not drunk. Just a lack of sleep."

The proprietor of the inn, Johnnie, came out of the passageway to the pantry. Spotting his only two customers, he came over, a towel over one shoulder.

"You boys need anything?" Johnnie asked.

Stephen's tongue caressed his teeth, not liking the metal taste. "What's cooking?"

"Hungry, eh?" Johnnie said. "It's not long to dinner."

"I was wondering if it was worth it to come back."

"It's always worth it." Johnnie grinned. "We've got eel stew in the pot and fresh round cakes and beans with cabbage."

"I like the sound of that," Stephen said.

"The eels or the cabbage?"

"Both." Stephen struggled to find a way to be subtle about the next thing he planned to say, but subtlety avoided him, so he just blurted out, "I hear you had a break-in of your strong room."

Johnnie's face went hard and remote. Clearly, it was something he neither wanted to be reminded of nor to discuss. "What of it?"

"Oh, just curious, I suppose. We wondered how it was possible, owing to the fact that careful innkeepers such as yourself guard their strong rooms well."

Johnnie's mouth turned down. "It happened during the night, when everyone was asleep. I had a dog on that floor, but she died during the night. That's the only reason why anyone got in."

"That is oddly fortuitous."

"We think she was poisoned," Johnnie said. "That's the only thing that makes sense. We found her on her back by the door in her usual place, some scraps about her, foam in her mouth."

"A pity about the dog."

"A pity about what was lost! Almost a hundred pounds in coin and jewelry — at least that's what the owners claimed. I'll be hearing from lawyers about it for ten years."

"Ah, lawyers. I hate lawyers. Nothing good ever happens when they come around."

"Damned right about that. Flies on shit, that's what they are. The only ones who weren't upset about it were those two." Johnnie waved toward the door.

"Who?"

"The fellows that just left. Philip Wyking and Richard Kilwardby. And they lost as much as anyone."

"Sorry to hear that. What were they out?"

"A chest of coin. Most of their takings from that week."

"Their takings?"

Johnnie pointed upwards. "They own the girls."

"You don't have your own whores?" Most innkeepers who allowed whores the run of the place owned them. It was unusual for that not to be the case.

"I do, but only two."

"I'll bet your girls didn't like it," Gilbert muttered.

Johnnie shot him a sharp look. "They do what they're told. Anyway, I've not laid them off. They're working the kitchen. I need the help there, with all the new custom."

"And having a jolly time of it, I imagine," Gilbert said.

"I don't understand why you'd put your girls aside," Stephen said.

"Those fellows made me an offer I couldn't refuse. More than my girls might bring in. They follow the king around from place to place. Make quite a good living at it, if what they paid me is any indication."

"Did any of the new girls put anything in the strong room?" Stephen asked.

Johnnie frowned. He was used to answering questions now and didn't seem to mind this one. "No. They have nothing of value of their own."

"I suppose they wouldn't have. Say, did you know Father Giles de Twet?"

"I knew him by sight. He's not the sort to speak much to me other than give a good day. Civil enough about it, but that was the extent of our conversations."

"Did he come in here often?"

"He did, a bit. Never seen a man with such a long face. Used to sit in a corner and drink himself to sleep."

"Any idea why?"

"God's hangnails! I said the man didn't speak to me."

"Did he enjoy any feminine companionship?"

"Course he did. Those hussies can't leave alone a man with coin."

"Did Father Giles favor any of them?"

Johnnie sneered. "Adeline, of course. She's the one reserved for the gentle lot."

"The girl who just went up with de Clare?"

"That was Adeline. I wouldn't mind an hour with her, but she wouldn't give me the time of day. She might you, though, if you're interested."

"Perhaps when she is free." Stephen rose. This time he was steady on his feet. "Tell me, did anyone ever find the pimps' chest?"

Johnnie opened and closed his mouth in a good imitation of a fish's. "You know, they did. It was in the church across the way. What's your interest in all this? It don't sound like a care for idle gossip."

"I'm just curious."

"Hmm," Johnnie grunted. He collected the empty pitcher and cups, and disappeared into the pantry at the rear of the inn.

Stephen paused at the foot of the stairs. The thought crossed his mind to use this moment to question one of the girls. There was that saucy red-head, Jennet, whom he wouldn't mind seeing again, even if it was only business.

But a fit, muscular man who had the hard look of a soldier stared at him from the top. One of the girl's minders? Probably so. There was no seeing any of the women alone, and none was likely to speak truthfully with the minder present.

Stephen nodded. The man returned the nod. Stephen turned away.

Chapter 14

The baggage train filled the street as it plodded south away from the castle and the marketplace.

Stephen and Gilbert sheltered against the side of the Golden Swan because soldiers assigned to guard the train marched on either side of the wagons so that there was no room left for ordinary people to go about their business against the massive flow.

At a break in the procession, Stephen grabbed Gilbert's collar and pulled him into the swarm.

"What are you doing?" Gilbert cried at being so roughly handled that he would have fallen if Stephen hadn't held him up. "Where are we going?"

"Not to worry," Stephen said as he pulled Gilbert along at a quick pace. "Not with them, for long anyway."

"But where?" Gilbert gasped.

"Seems to me we should talk to that fellow Robbie."

"What fellow Robbie? I don't remember such a fellow."

"We were given his name as the sergeant of the gate."

"Oh, that Robbie. Of course, him. I was about to suggest as much since we appear to be at loose ends."

"I accept your suggestion."

"I wish you accepted all of them."

"Except that you're not always right."

"I am so! Half the time, anyway. The important half."

Stephen remembered that Robbie's house was the last on the right in Morstreet. He stepped out of the procession at that house and stood at the edge of a weed-choked ditch, beyond which a field of winter rye had been planted, the sprouts frail and green.

A woman with a face lined from toil and exposure to the sun stood behind a wattle fence with two girls about seven or eight who were watching the baggage train as it passed by and drew out of sight on the road toward Stanes. A kettle steamed over a fire behind them. The woman took up a long-handled paddle and dipped it into the kettle.

"Come on, girls," the woman said. "Fun's over. Back to work. The laundry won't do itself."

As the girls reluctantly took up their paddles, Stephen said, "Excuse me, I'm looking for someone name of Robbie. He's a sergeant-of-the-watch at the castle. I'm told he lives here."

The woman ceased stirring the laundry. "Yea, that may be true. What do you want him for?" she asked suspiciously

"Just for a few questions," Stephen said. "I'm not a bill collector or anything like that, if that's what worries you."

"So you say," the woman said, holding her paddle as a weapon in case she needed to run Stephen off.

"I swear," Stephen said. "I've just a few questions about his job and what he might have seen of Father Giles."

The woman frowned. "The one who they found in the river?"

The girls' eyes grew round at this suggestion that a matter of community significance such as the Father's murder might have touched their household in some way.

"Back in a moment." She leaned her paddle against a bench and went into the house.

She came out shortly with a balding man with grey hair, although he didn't really look that old. A girl of twelve or so filled the doorway; she wore an apron that was spotted with burned marks from tending the fire: the household cook?

"My wife says you've questions about Father Giles," Robbie said. "Don't know that I can help you much."

"I understand you were sergeant of the first night watch on the evening Father Giles disappeared," Stephen said.

"Yea, that and the last watch."

"You saw him leave through the barbican?"

"I did."

"What time was it?'

"The sun had just gone down. A nearly quarter moon was high."

"The light was good, then?"

"Good enough."

"Did you see where he went after leaving the castle?"

"He went through the marketplace. This was a Saturday, mind, and there were a few vendors who hadn't finished packing up. He stopped at a couple of them."

"Did he buy anything?"

"No, he looked a bit at what was left. Then he walked on."

"Did you see where he went after that?"

"Oh, sure. The church."

"You're sure about that? Didn't the vendors in the market block the view?"

"I was at the top of Salisbury Tower." At Stephen's puzzled look, Robbie added, "It's the one at the southwest corner of the lower bailey. I like to take the view from there after the watch is set."

"Can you see the Golden Swan from the tower?"

"Oh, yes."

"And he went into the church? Not into the Swan?"

"Well, he turned aside toward the church."

"You can't see the doors from the tower?"

"No, the houses in Draper's Row are in the way."

"Did you happen to see anything else of interest?"

"Nah." Robbie frowned. "Except at the same time Father Giles went into the church, there were two fellows who came out of the Swan and crossed the street toward it. Couldn't tell if they went in. Didn't think anything of it at the time. Is it important?"

"Only time will tell. Did you happen to mention any of this to Sir Adam Rykelyng?"

"Never spoke to the man, or anyone else who isn't part of my shift, about it."

"So much for the thoroughness of Sir Adam's investigation," Gilbert murmured.

"What?" Robbie asked.

"Nothing," Gilbert said. "It's nothing. Just an idle thought. I have them all the time. So bothersome."

The Golden Swan was serving dinner when Stephen and Gilbert returned. But it was not as crowded as they had seen it in the past, and most of those filling the tables looked like shopkeepers and craftsmen of the town rather than soldiers.

Stephen and Gilbert settled down at a table by the back wall and ordered a round of eel soup and fried cabbage with turnips and onions, washed down with weak ale.

The girls loitered near the stairway and did not make much of an effort to attract business. Now and then one or another showed some bosom or leg to one of the guests, accompanied by a bored expression. A few of the targets sauntered over and they and a girl climbed the stairs to the chambers above to take care of business. Many of the targets did not take long at it, but then, they were working men and had to get back to their shops, for the winter days were short. Dallying over dessert could mean missed business.

Stephen caught Jennet's eye when she came back down. She beckoned with a shrug of her shoulder.

"I'll be back in a little bit," Stephen said, wiping his mouth on his napkin.

Gilbert glanced from Stephen to Jennet. He nodded and waved for more soup.

Jennet led Stephen by the hand to a chamber at the rear of the building overlooking a courtyard.

"My humble abode," she said as she held the door for him to enter.

It was a typical inn chamber, a bed wide enough for two (or three in a pinch) without curtains. Stephen settled on the mattress, which crinkled and pricked his arse: filled with straw.

Jennet knelt before him and started to untie Stephen's stockings. He grasped her hands and lifted her to sit beside him.

"What?" Jennet asked. "You fancy something other than the usual?"

"Something else, yes."

She regarded him narrowed eyes. "I'll not take it in the bung, nor submit to tying up or beating, if that's your preference in amusement."

"I have something else in mind."

"Such as? A good cry on my shoulder and a pat on the head? Those are available, too."

"I wouldn't mind that. Maybe later. First, I have some questions."

Jennet was quiet for a moment. "Like what — what's my real name? How did I sink to this life of sin?"

"You can tell me your story some other time. I'm interested in a customer here. His name was Father Giles."

Jennet paled at the mention of Giles' name. She fumbled behind her for a bell that hung by a cord from the bedpost. She rang the bell and shouted, "Bill! I've got a problem!"

Feet thundered outside and the door burst open. A very large man stepped into the room, slapping a nasty looking club into one massive hand. It was the same fellow Stephen had seen earlier at the top of the stairs.

"Hello, Bill," Stephen said. "How're you doing?"

Bill did not reply. He grasped Stephen by the coat collar and lifted him off the bed to such a height that Stephen's feet did not touch the floor. Stephen kicked at Bill's groin, but this was a task Bill obviously had performed many times; he anticipated the kick and easily avoided it. He shook Stephen like a handful of rags.

"Careful, there, Bill," Stephen said. "You might break something."

Bill's reply was to fling Stephen through the door. He collided with the far wall outside with an impact as bad as falling from the back of a galloping horse and slid to the floor. His shoulder hurt like the devil, but he did not think anything had broken.

Bill strode out of the chamber, his booted feet stamping on the floorboards so that the entire inn seemed to tremble. He reached for Stephen again.

Stephen held up a hand. "I'm finished, Bill. I'll go. No need to rip my head off. Although I'm sure you'd enjoy it, there would be repercussions, you know."

"Let him go, Bill. He's connected," Jennet said.

Bill stayed his hand, and Stephen climbed to his feet, his shoulder twanging.

"I'll see myself out, thank you very much," Stephen said.

When Stephen tottered down the stairs to the hall, he looked at the table he and Gilbert had occupied. But Gilbert was not there, and a servant was clearing away the trenchers, bowls and cups.

"Where's the other fellow who was here?" Stephen asked the servant.

"Arrested," the servant replied, loading the remains of Stephen's dinner onto a wooden tray.

"What do you mean, arrested!?" Stephen said.

"That's what I said. Three unpleasant fellows came in, saw him, and hauled him away. He didn't pay up. Are you going to take care of that?" The servant held out his hand.

Stephen put money in the waiting palm. "Did they actually say Gilbert was under arrest?"

"That was his name? No, they didn't, now that you mention it. They just saw him, spoke among themselves a moment, and dragged him off. I figured it was an arrest. Are they looking for you, too?"

"You have never looked upon a more law-abiding man," Stephen said.

"You know, something makes me doubt that."

Gilbert was lost. There was nothing Stephen could do for him. It was a bitter realization, but he couldn't afford to linger on it. The men who had taken Gilbert could only have been FitzAllan retainers. As soon as they got Gilbert alone, they would pound Ida's hiding place out of him. He had to get to

159

Ida before Gilbert gave up her location. Otherwise, he would lose her, too.

Gilbert would give him time to get to her. He would hold out for a little while, then he would tell what he knew.

Stephen's first impulse was to race up Morstreet. But more FitzAllan men could be wandering around there.

He turned from the inn's front door and hurried toward the rear. He was aware of Philip Wyking and Richard Kilwardby following his progress, but he could no more spare a thought for them than he could for Gilbert.

He went past the kitchen, pantry and buttery and out the back door to the courtyard. There did not seem to be a break to a back garden, so he tried the door on a room at the back wing of the inn. It was not locked. He entered and found it deserted. He opened the window and climbed out.

There was no break for access to a back garden because the inn had no garden, just an indentation between the fenced gardens of its neighbors that sloped down to a field where sheep grazed on stubble. The sheep turned to face him in a line, waiting to see what Stephen would do.

"I come in peace," Stephen cautioned as he slipped to the path behind the back gardens of the houses on Morstreet. He hoped there wasn't a ram among them. It was not a pleasant experience to be knocked off your feet by a ram who was feeling protective.

He reached the path and passed along it without retaliation from the sheep and within moments was behind the houses along Peascod Street.

The houses ran down Peascod Street for about two-hundred yards or so before the town came to a halt. Stephen crossed the street where they ended and passed around behind those on the other side of the street. The ground was marshy here, a drainage ditch running down from the houses to a small pond, where several boys could be seen fishing from the bank.

Stephen stayed on course behind the houses until he found an alley that opened onto Newstreet, which ran down to the river where the ferryboats crossed.

He paused at the top of Newstreet, and scanned up and down Morstreet. There were people about, but no one he recognized, not that he was likely to know a FitzAllan face. He'd seen quite a few of them a while back when he was a prisoner at the earl's castle at Clun, but that seemed long ago now and he couldn't remember what any of them looked like.

There was nothing for it but to take the leap. So, he set off down the hill toward the bridge, half expecting voices to cry out in alarm at his back.

But he made the turn toward the bridge, where the chapel lay, without a challenge. Only a woman emerging from a bakehouse a short distance from the turn paid him any mind, for she smiled back at him when their eyes met as he went by.

He turned down the street that led to the hovels that made up the district of Underore and hurried beyond a large slaughterhouse to their barn, which was some distance away, but not far enough to insulate it entirely from the bad smells of the slaughterhouse, of cow manure, rot and decay, which mingled with the eyewatering reek of urine from its neighboring tanneries.

Despite the bad smells, Ida was on a bench by the barn where they had spent the night when Stephen stumbled up.

"What is it?" she asked in alarm.

"FitzAllan's men have taken Gilbert," Stephen panted. "We have to get away. They could be here any moment."

"They will torture him?" Ida asked anxiously as they crossed the race of the town's mill and turned to make their way along a narrow, churned up lane toward the bridge, she on Gilbert's mule and Stephen on his mare.

"He'll hold out for a time, long enough for me to get you away to somewhere safe, then he'll confess what he knows," Stephen said.

"Poor Gilbert! Was there nothing you could do for him?"

"Not and get you away."

"I hate to think he must suffer for me."

"I hate the thought, too, but it cannot be helped. He is a prisoner of his circumstances, as we are."

They came onto the street at the head of the bridge. Ida paused the mule.

"That way," Stephen said, pointing to the bridge, thinking she did not know where he intended to go. "Across the bridge."

"And that way is to the castle." Ida pointed toward the massive white fortification looming above them.

She pressed her heels to the mule and turned it toward the castle.

"What are you doing?" Stephen asked.

"I will not let that little man be tortured to protect me," she said grimly.

They had no trouble getting into the castle, since the gate wardens knew Stephen at least by name. But Ida got odd looks since she was dressed like a common girl and riding a mule instead of walking.

When they reached the upper bailey, Ida turned aside to the courtyard of the king's hall.

"FitzAllan will be in there, with Edward, I have no doubt," Ida said as she dismounted. "He sticks to the prince like a flea does a rat."

The hall was empty, except for a gathering of noblemen about Prince Edward at the other end by a great fireplace.

Ida marched across the hall. A couple of servants swerved to intercept her, since common girls were not allowed in the hall, much less to approach the royal person of Prince Edward. But Stephen fended them off.

Edward, who was bending over a large parchment map spread upon the table, looked up as they drew near.

"Attebrook, what are you doing here?" Edward asked, removing his finger from the map where he had been pointing to something of interest and murmuring things that should be done about it. "Have you something to report? Can't it wait?"

"Sir Stephen is not here for any business you have put upon him, your grace," Ida said. "He is here on my behalf."

"And you are?" Edward asked, puzzled and impatient at this interruption.

"I am Ida Attebrook of Hafton Manor, your grace," she said. "Until a short time ago, I was FitzAllan's prisoner."

"His prisoner?" Edward said. He turned to FitzAllan, who was only a step away. "Isn't this the ward you spoke about? The one who disappeared?"

"She is, your grace," FitzAllan said with a predatory smile.

"I am no man's ward, your grace," Ida said. "And I have come to demand that Gilbert Wistwode will not be harmed on my account."

Edward smiled faintly. "How are you not a ward?"

"Because Sir Stephen carried me off to London where we were made man and wife."

Chapter 15

Edward put a finger to his mouth. "If what the lady says is true, you were quite the busy man in London, Attebrook — arrested, breaking gaol, and somehow finding the time to wed. Quite a lot of work in such a short time." He leaned forward and added with menace, "So, is it true? Did you wed her?"

If Stephen thought back at the Golden Swan that the world was spinning apart, that distress was nothing to what he felt now. Yet he knew he could not show how he felt. He glanced at Ida, who stood with her head high, narrow nostrils flared, lips a thin line, the picture of defiance. Whatever Stephen said, he would be damned. Say one thing and Ida was lost. Say another, and he played the prince false, for which he would never be forgiven if found out. The question welling in his mind was, which damnation would he choose?

"It is true, your grace," Stephen said. "I married her."

"This is preposterous!" FitzAllan cried. "The girl is his niece!"

"Not niece of the blood," Ida said. "I am my father's step-daughter. I share no blood with my husband!"

"I cannot believe this!" FitzAllan thundered. "It is a lie!"

"Have me examined," Ida snapped. "I am not a virgin."

"I will have the proof," FitzAllan declared. "Summon the wise women to have a look at her."

"Bring them on," Ida said. "You will be disappointed."

"It is still a marriage forbidden by the church," FitzAllan said.

"Then let the church unravel it," Ida said. "That will take years."

Edward regarded Stephen and Ida. His expression was unfriendly, and so was his tone when he spoke. "I am inclined to think that you *have* married her, Attebrook. One might think it solves the problem of who holds the right to that manor without the crown's determination. And it would appear to moot the question of whether she is a royal ward. Bold move."

"Damn your bones, Attebrook!" FitzAllan shouted. He slammed his hand on the tabletop, causing everyone but Stephen and Edward to jerk with surprise. "I will see you ruined! I will see you dead!"

"And yet you have failed so far," Stephen said. "Despite numerous attempts."

"We'll have no threats made around this table," Edward said. "We have a war to fight, gentlemen, and I will not stand for my supporters, whether they are high or low, going at each other's throats. Look to the throats of our enemies if you want blood." He turned aside and drew FitzAllan away. "I will find a way to compensate you for your loss," Stephen heard the prince murmur to FitzAllan.

FitzAllan trembled with fury for a moment. Then he nodded, but not without throwing a venomous glare at Stephen.

"About the question of Gilbert Wistwode, your grace!" Ida called.

"Who is he?" Edward asked.

"He is Sir Stephen's loyal man, and my friend. The earl's men have him in hold. I would ask, in your mercy, that he be released immediately."

"Well, FitzAllan?" Edward asked.

"I know nothing of it. But if it's true, I'll have it undone."

Chapter 16

"Are you angry with me?" Ida asked as they reached the courtyard.

"There is no word to describe how I feel," Stephen said. "Poleaxed is the best I can think of."

"I couldn't think of anything else to do," she said.

"You could at least have warned me first."

"Well, you would have raised all sorts of objections."

"You have that right."

They walked through the gate into the bailey.

"Did what we say amount to the saying of the words?" Ida asked.

Stephen paused, hands behind his back, head down. "All it takes is a declaration of an intention to marry by the parties involved. A lawyer could defend what we have just done as making a marriage. Especially in front of those witnesses."

He walked on toward the mare and Gilbert's mule. "It doesn't matter so much to us. But it could be a problem down the road to the children of our true marriages. It could interfere with them inheriting whatever property we eventually leave behind us, if they are deemed bastards."

"I had not thought of that," Ida said.

"Well, we might get an annulment at some point. Although those are expensive, and as you mentioned, can take years to acquire."

Ida smiled slightly, looking away across the bailey. "It's good to have a husband who's a lawyer. That might save some on the expense of the annulment."

"I am not and never was a lawyer," Stephen said, thinking about his years as one Ademar de Valence's law clerks. "I was barely a decent scrivener."

"But you sound convincing. Isn't that what matters most?"

"It matters, but that's not all there is to it."

"There is a bright side. At least you and Mistress Bartelot are relieved of the burden of finding me a husband. For now, anyway."

"That *is* a weight off my mind. What happened to Mistress Bartelot, anyway?" Stephen asked. Mistress Bartelot, a severe woman with a strong sense of rectitude, was the original tenant in the house he now occupied in Ludlow across from the Broken Shield Inn. He had allowed her to remain, since she had nowhere to go when he took over, and she had been abducted with Ida to serve as her maid. He felt badly that he had not asked about her until now.

"FitzAllan sent her home."

"She is safe, then?"

"As I am at the moment. Thanks to you."

"Time will tell how safe you are."

Ida laughed. "Life around you turns out to be filled with danger. Perhaps I should run away and pretend that none of this has happened."

"There is your mule," Stephen said. "I don't know how far you are likely to get on him, though."

"I would not want to deprive Gilbert of his beloved." She glanced sideways at Stephen. "Besides, I should have a horse of my own. It won't do to have your wife riding pillion behind you all the time, or walking."

"God's knuckles, married less than a quarter hour and you're already making demands."

"That's what wives do, don't they? Nag their husbands into doing what they ought?"

Stephen cupped his hands into a makeshift stirrup. "Let me help you up, wife. We need to get back to the barn. That's where Gilbert will go after they release him."

Gilbert turned up at the barn an hour later with a split lip and a black eye.

"It's a good thing you acted so quickly," he said, pressing the sides of his broad nose as if to check whether it was still straight, although there was no sign of injury; it was as broad and flat as usual. "They were about to start breaking my fingers. Not that I would have minded much, though I am rather fond of them. How ever did you manage it? Black magic?

"Worse," Stephen said. "We declared before Prince Edward that we married in London. As a married woman, she cannot be FitzAllan's ward."

"You married?" Gilbert said, finding his nose intact and settling onto the bench outside the barn. "I hadn't noticed. When did that happen?"

"Well, you weren't always paying attention," Ida said.

"Small things do escape my attention now and then," Gilbert said. "But this seems like a rather large thing."

"It was either that or your broken fingers," Stephen said. "And perhaps after that, your head."

"I am grateful for that," Gilbert said. "But still. It was rash. Not a thing easily undone if it is held to be true. And I am hurt that you didn't invite me to be a witness."

"There wasn't time. A spur of the moment decision."

"Really?"

"It was Ida's idea," Stephen said.

"She proposed to you, eh?"

"I wouldn't call it a proposal, exactly," Stephen said. "It felt more like a blow upon the head."

"It was all I could manage under the circumstances," Ida said. "You did rise well to the occasion, though."

"Stephen, a married man," Gilbert mused. "Great Saint Cuthbert's nostrils, the next thing and you'll settle down and give up your life of crime and misadventure. It will be England's loss, but one must expect change, I suppose."

Ida, who was seated next to Stephen, took his arm. "I shall steer him to the right path."

"I hope you have better luck than Harry and me," Gilbert said. "God knows, we tried. Or I did. Harry is more a corrupting influence."

Ida twisted Stephen's ear, but not hard. "You just haven't tried the right way." She let go of the ear. "Now, husband, are you going to make me languish another night in this foul-smelling place? Surely your wife deserves a better bed than a lump of straw in a drafty barn."

Stephen pointed a finger at Ida. "See what she has become in only an hour? She demanded I buy her a horse already."

"I told you she wouldn't like our commodious barn," Gilbert laughed. "Now that you are on the hook, you have no choice but to obey."

Stephen chuckled and stood up. He extended a hand to Ida. "Come. I don't care to spend the night in this barn, either."

The inn Stephen selected was the Wily Minstrel, which was by the Thames bridge. He thought it best to find a place away from the market and Morstreet where FitzAllan's adherents might be encountered.

The chamber given to Stephen and Ida was on the second floor. It had a window overlooking the town wharf and the river. Stephen threw open the shutters so they could look at the water and bridge arching to the other shore. The wind was blowing out of the west, so the air smelled fresh, lacking the stink of the tanneries and the slaughterhouse to the east.

"We must share the room?" Ida asked. She didn't say anything about the bed, for there was only one. They would address that problem when the time came.

"It will be awkward," Stephen said. "But we must maintain the pretense."

"Yes, we must."

"It would be best if you don't go out. Or if you do, don't go up the hill. I think it will be safe enough for you down here and in Eatun."

"Yes."

Stephen crossed to the door.

"Where are you off to?" Ida asked. She smiled wanly. "Just asking as a neglected wife."

"To put the business of Father Giles behind us, so we can go home."

Chapter 17

Stephen hesitated on the threshold of the hall in the castle's upper bailey. He dreaded going in, but he felt he had no choice.

Gilbert stirred at his elbow.

"You can wait out here if you like," Stephen said. "If lightning strikes me, you'll be missed."

"Are you sure you don't mind? After what you told me of the previous interview, I have to admit I am rather worried."

"You look a sight, anyway. You'll just remind everyone of the unpleasantness."

Gilbert looked relieved. "And you won't? It would be a shame to make a widow of Lady Ida on her wedding day."

"I don't know. She'll probably be glad to be rid of me in the long run."

He went in. The conference had broken up, probably long ago, and there were only four men sitting on padded chairs by the fire blazing in the great fireplace. Stephen took a deep breath and marched up to them.

One of those enjoying the fire's warmth was Edward. He caught sight of Stephen, looked annoyed, and ignored him.

"Excuse me, my lords," Stephen said. "I would like to speak with his grace's deputy. Could you tell me where I might find him?"

A slender handsome man in his fifties with gray and brown hair who bore a worrisome resemblance to King Henry perked up. "What do you want, Attebrook? Have you brought us more trouble?"

"I am afraid so, my lord."

"That's Earl Richard of Cornwall to you."

"My apologies, your grace," Stephen said hastily. He got the significance of the resemblance now: the earl was the king's younger brother. Sovereigns were prickly about their pride, but their younger brothers could be even worse. "I did not realize it was you."

"Get on with it. I will do well enough for a deputy. What bad news do you have for us to disturb this pleasant afternoon?"

"I have reason to believe that a spy ring is operating in the town. Its object is to learn of your war plans."

"War plans!" Edward said sharply. "I have no war plans!"

"I have heard you have such plans, your grace, and no doubt the spies have heard it, too," Stephen said. "There has been talk about them at the Golden Swan."

One of the others by the fire was Gilbert de Clare. He paled at the mention of the Golden Swan and war plans, and terror crossed his face for moment before a bland mask descended. Stephen did not meet his eye and pretended he had not noticed de Clare.

Edward pounded the arm of his chair. "God's knees!" he shouted. "I can't take a piss without Montfort hearing of it!" He turned on Stephen. "Just what do these spies know?"

"I can't tell you that, your grace, without questioning them."

"And to do that, we need to have them arrested," Edward growled, the realization of why Stephen had come back dawning. "My lord earl, will you please take care of this matter?"

"Of course," Earl Richard said.

Soldiers were mustering in the lower bailey, thirty of them. Earl Richard wanted to plug all escape routes and ensure that he had all members of the ring in the bag.

Gilbert de Clare paused at Stephen's side. "What do you intend to say to them about me?" he asked quietly at Stephen's shoulder.

"What is there to say about you, my lord?" Stephen asked, not turning his head. "The woman used you like she used many innocent others. So, as far as I am concerned, you were never there."

"I am grateful for this, Attebrook. I will not forget it."

"Your servant, my lord. Oh, there is one thing."

"What?" de Clare asked suspiciously.

"Did Adeline or any of the other girls ever mention Father Giles' name to you?"

"No," de Clare said, puzzled. "Never."

Ten soldiers led by Rykelyng's younger brother Ernulf left the castle on horseback. They turned down Peascod Street without attracting any undue attention. With the little army there, the comings and goings of soldiers were so common that no one noticed much, other than to get out of the way.

The objective of this contingent was to get around behind the Golden Swan to prevent any of the quarry from escaping out the back as Stephen had done.

After an interval that Sir Adam Rykelyng, the officer in command, judged that enough time had passed for the backstop to get into place, he led the remainder plus Stephen on foot to the Swan. Rykelyng directed ten of that number through the arched gateway to the courtyard, while one of the other ten held open the door to the inn and the rest, led by Rykelyng and Stephen, went inside.

There were only a few people at the tables, and no women in sight.

"Are they here?" Rykelyng asked Stephen, referring to Philip Wyking, Richard Kilwardby and the hulk, Bill.

"No," Stephen said. "Have the men check upstairs."

Rykelyng waved at the stairway, and all the soldiers thundered upward.

Johnnie, alerted by the commotion, came out from the rear of the inn. "What's going on, sirs?" he asked, watching the last of the soldiers vanish into the first floor.

"We are looking for three men, Wyking, Kilwardby and a fellow known only to us as Bill," Rykelyng said.

Johnnie bobbed his head. "You've just missed them by no more than an hour, sir."

"What do you mean?" Rykelyng demanded.

"They've gone, sir," Johnnie said. "Left."

"The women, too?" Rykelyng asked.

"Why, yes. In haste, too. They'd paid up for the rest of the week."

"Where did they go?" Stephen asked.

"I don't know, sir," Johnnie said. "I was in the back. They didn't say nothing to me. One of my girls told me they were leaving."

"Pardon me if I don't take your word for it," Rykelyng said. "We'll continue searching."

"Please don't break anything, sir," Johnnie said plaintively, an indication that he did not have much hope the searchers would be kind to his property.

Rykelyng did not reply.

"Which girl brought word to you?" Stephen asked Johnnie.

"It was Henrietta," Johnnie said.

"Where is she now?"

"In the kitchen."

"Please fetch her here."

"At once."

Johnnie hurried into the rear of the inn and came out a few moments later with a lanky girl as tall as many men. She had a jutting chin, full lips and mousy brown hair falling from her linen cap.

"You are Henrietta?" Stephen asked the woman.

"I am, sir. Can I be of service?"

"What do you know about the departure of Wyking, Kilwardby, Bill and their women?" Stephen asked.

Henrietta licked her lips. "I heard them arguing, the men that is. Wyking said they had been found out and they had to flee for their lives. The other two, they didn't agree. They thought things were fine."

"What do you mean, found out?"

"It was you, sir, that set them off — when you tried to question that one girl, the red-haired one, about Father Giles. Wyking was sure you were on to their scheme or soon would be, what with all the questions you were asking. He said it was better to be safe than sorry, and convinced the others to go."

"What scheme was that?"

"Gathering information from the soldiers who come here."

"You knew about that?" Rykelyng asked harshly.

"I got eyes and ears, sir," Henrietta stammered. "I can piece things together. Those girls, they asked an uncommon lot of questions. Stuff we working girls don't usually ask about, like plans and numbers of men and where they'd come from and who their leaders were and the like."

"And you said nothing?" Rykelyng said.

"I was afraid, sir," Henrietta said. "They're hard men, they are. They'd have killed me soon as look at me, if they knew what I thought." She shivered. "That Bill, especially. He was a mean one."

"Let her go, Rykelyng," Stephen said.

"You believe me, don't you, sir?" Henrietta implored.

"I do," Stephen said, although he had doubts. It could be Henrietta sympathized with the barons' faction; many people in this area of the country did. But it was not worth pursuing her. "Now, tell me, did you see which way they went?"

"I saw them turn their wagon south out the gate, sir."

Was she telling the truth? Stephen decided she was.

Stephen said to Rykelyng. "If we hurry, we might still catch them."

There was, in fact, a back door to the Swan that opened into the fields to the west. Rykelyng and Stephen went through it. They ejected two of the soldiers from their horses, and led the rest at a fast canter along the backs of the houses until they came to a gap on Sheetstreet where they were able to get through to Morstreet.

Sheetstreet diverged from Morstreet at a fork. The spies could have taken either fork. If the pursuers guessed wrong, there was no chance of catching them.

The Corpse at Windsor Bridge

But a set of stocks stood at the crossroad which was occupied by an elderly man whose long white hair stood out about his head as if driven by the wind, although it was an uncommonly calm and sunny day, the sky having cleared after last night's rain.

"Did you see a wagon bearing three men and six or seven women pass by here not long ago?" Stephen asked the elderly man.

"Why, I could hardly miss them, could I, sir, save if I'd fallen asleep, which is a bit hard in this contraption," he said.

"Which way did they go?"

"That way," the old man said, pointing toward Morstreet.

"Many thanks to you," Stephen said.

"Say, you couldn't pause to put in a good word with the bailiffs, could you? I'd like to get out of here!" the old man called as the soldiers trotted away. "What's the hurry!"

Stephen took the lead and set a hard pace.

The little village of Old Windsor, just a few hovels at a crossroad a couple of miles from the castle, quickly came and went. A pack of boys playing with a hoop in the street confirmed that a wagon with three men and a number of women had passed through a short time ago.

Stephen pressed on, the others straggling behind, as the setting sun cast long shadows across the road and a pure golden light painted the fields and the billowing clouds above his head. There was hardly an hour of daylight remaining. Would the spies find a place to lay up for the night? Somewhere off the road and out of sight?

A dense forest closed in on the road a short distance out of Old Windsor. The grey branches entangling overhead made for a gloomy ride.

Stephen glanced into the forest on either side of the road, looking for signs the quarry had pulled off, since it was the time when any traveler stopped to feed and water the horses, and to set up what camp he could beneath his wagon. But there was no sign along the way that a wagon had pressed into the forest.

A road loomed on the right. Sunbeams draped across the road like curtains, growing thicker and more substantial.

Sunbeams depended on dust floating in the air. Stephen saw that dust suspended above the road, trapped by the overhanging branches even though the leaves had long since fallen.

Something or someone had passed by here not long before and stirred up the dust.

The dust grew ever thicker.

And then ahead he saw it: a large wagon.

"I think that's them," Stephen said over his shoulder. "Make ready." He drew his sword and swung his borrowed shield off his back.

He was no more than a hundred yards behind the wagon. He pressed the horse into a gallop and relished the surge as she bolted forward.

Figures in the wagon spotted Stephen's onrush. Voices shouted ahead. The figures scrambled for things in the bed of the wagon. The man astride the leading horse on the left side lashed the four-horse team into a gallop.

Stephen was fifty yards away, forty, thirty ....

The figures had resolved long since into two men and several women. Stephen recognized Bill and the other man, Wyking or Kilwardby. Their faces were intent and not frightened. Adeline was beside Bill.

She and another woman raised crossbows at the same moment the men raised and drew bows.

Time slowed down. It could only have been a brief span, but it felt as though it stretched for minutes, as Adeline squinted over the top of the crossbow and the men drew to the corners of their mouths.

They loosed and the arrows flew.

Three whirred by Stephen's head. He heard shouts.

But he could not pay attention to what damage had occurred behind.

Adeline's quarrel had struck Stephen's horse. It reared and bucked, shrieking, and it was all he could do to stay on.

The horse settled as Stephen dug into her sides, urging her forward before those in the wagon could shoot again.

But he was not in time.

He was almost close enough to strike those in the wagon when Adeline shot again, aiming for the horse.

The quarrel slammed into the horse's breast and this time she took two strides and went down as if struck upon the head.

Stephen pitched forward as the horse collapsed. He watched the ground approaching. He threw up his hands to break the fall and rolled with the impact, the horse's hindquarters slamming into the earth inches away.

He rolled on down the road, striking his head hard on the ground.

He lay still, his body a mass of pain, although it was a dull pain and not as great as he thought it might be. He waited for the greater pain to come, the pain that would tell him that he had broken something.

Yet, no such pain arrived.

He sat up and looked about.

The wagon had vanished in the distance.

Five horses were down, and another three had been wounded. Four men had fallen and were not moving. Two were getting to their feet.

Rykelyng was one of those getting to his feet. Blood ran down his face from a cut over an eye. He knelt by one of the fallen men. It was his brother, Ernulf. He touched Ernulf's face, then fixed his bloody eye on Stephen.

"He's dead, you stupid, reckless bastard," Rykelyng hissed. "This is your doing!"

Chapter 18

Ernulf was the only man dead. Three other men were injured, one with a broken arm, another with a shoulder dislocation, and the third with a back injury that made it painful for him to sit up.

They loaded the man with the shoulder dislocation and back injury on one of the horses and the dead man on the other, and walked back to Windsor.

It was a couple hours after dark by the time they arrived. Rykelyng halted the men on the street before the church of Saint John the Baptist across from the Golden Swan.

"We'll put Ernulf in there until the morrow when he can be buried," Rykelyng said.

Stephen approached the horse carrying the corpse.

"Not you," Rykelyng snapped. "You'll not touch him."

Stephen stepped back while two of the soldiers eased the dead man down. He followed them as they carried him to the church.

But Rykelyng stopped him at the door. "Fetch the priest. Tell him we've brought Ernulf to be blessed and buried."

"Where will he be this time of night?" Stephen asked.

Rykelyng spat. "He's a house across the street on the back side of the church."

He turned away and entered the church.

Stephen groped his way around the side of the church, the graveyard stretching away to the south, marked here and there by faintly seen stones. The night was dark, but clear and starry through gathering clouds, with no moon yet.

A lane lined with houses lay ahead. It was impossible to tell which one belonged to the priest. Stephen chose a house at random and pounded on the door. The owner opened a window on the first floor above his head.

"What the devil do you want this time of night?" the owner barked.

Stephen backed up so he could be seen. "I'm looking for the priest."

"Two doors down. Can't you see the sign?"

"Why are people so stupid?" remarked a woman in the room overhead.

"I don't know." The householder slammed the shutter closed.

"I should have known that. Sorry," Stephen muttered. He could just make out a white cross nailed to the post by the door of the indicated house.

He repeated the pounding on the front door at the house with the cross. There was no immediate response, so he continued pounding until a small window in the door at the height of an ordinary man's face, which is to say it was at the height of Stephen's shoulder, opened inward. The wheezy voice of an elderly man inquired in weary, patient tones from within the opaque hole, "Who are you and what is your business?"

Stephen bent to speak into the window. "I am Stephen Attebrook. There's been a mishap on the road. A knight of the prince's household has died. His companions have laid him in the church. The leader said I was to fetch you."

"Oh, dear. Of course. I shall be right there."

Some time passed before the priest appeared. He handed Stephen a tinderbox. "Would you mind carrying this? There's such a good chance I'll drop it in the dark."

Stephen accepted the metal box. It was warm from the coals within it even through the towel wrapped around it.

"How long has the poor man been dead?" the priest asked as they negotiated their way through the graveyard.

"Two hours, I'd say, give or take," Stephen said.

The priest sighed. "Too late for the *Viaticum*, I'm afraid. Well, I shall do what I can for him, poor man."

They reached the front door and stopped.

"Would you be so kind, young man, as to fetch a candle from the rack?" the priest asked.

"Of course, Father."

Stephen set down the tinderbox, slipped in and fumbled for the rack of votive candles by the door. He hesitated about taking one and fumbled some more about the rack for the jar that should be there with unused candles, but he could not find it. So, he gave in and reluctantly appropriated a used candle from the rack.

"Who's that?" Rykelyng called from within the church, which was so dark that neither he nor the other soldiers could be seen.

"Just me," Stephen said.

"I told you not to come in."

No, you didn't say that; although you may think you implied it, Stephen thought.

He said, "The priest requires a candle. He's waiting for it outside."

"Hurry up with it, then."

Stephen retreated to the doorway with his candle. He knelt and applied the wick to the glowing coals within the box. He shielded the flame from any breeze that might try to extinguish it, and handed it to the priest.

"There you go, Father," Stephen said.

"Thank you, my son."

The priest shuffled in.

Stephen shut the door.

The breeze freshened, bringing with it the delicate aroma of a pig sty.

He heard voices within the church, but the door was thick wood and the walls solid stone, so he could not make out what was said. One voice, which sounded like that of the elderly priest, predominated, though. He could have been saying prayers — Stephen thought that the ritual of Prayers for the Dead was most likely.

After a long while the door opened and the priest came out, followed by Rykelyng and the others. No one paid attention to Stephen but the priest, who touched Stephen's arm.

"Would you mind seeing me home, young man?" the priest asked.

"Certainly," Stephen said.

Rykelyng and the soldiers went toward Morstreet while Stephen took the tinderbox in one hand and the priest's elbow in the other so he might not trip in the tall grass as he had almost done on the way to the church.

"Father, do you remember a chest being found in the church about three weeks ago?" Stephen asked. "It would have been a Sunday, the day after the Conception of the Virgin."

"I do, indeed! There was a robbery at the Golden Swan that night! Someone broke into the strong room and made off with several chests of valuables. It caused such a scandal."

"There was only the one chest here, though?"

"Only the one."

They swerved around a gravestone.

"Nothing in it?"

"Picked as clean as a Christmas swan."

"The church was open, as it was tonight?"

"I never lock it. I like to leave it open for people who might have a need."

"You don't worry about the vestments? The cups and pitchers?"

"All the valuables are kept in my house."

"Did you happen to check on the church that night?"

"No, I usually have no reason to poke around after dark. Anyway, I like to get to bed early. I have a habit of waking in the night. Does sleeplessness trouble you?"

"No, not really."

"You are a lucky man."

"Did you waken that night?"

"I waken practically every night. It is a heaven-sent night if I sleep through it."

"Did you happen to hear or see anything unusual that night?"

"If you're talking about the robbery, no." The priest was silent as they reached the lane and stepped into it. "There was only one thing. It had nothing to do with the robbery — just some discourse between a man and his wife. Or at least I took them to be man and wife, although in this town, you can't always be sure about a couple out at that hour."

"What hour was that?"

"Very late. The moon was down by then."

Stephen looked up at the sky. The moon, still not visible, would rise later as a thin waning crescent. Three weeks ago, it would have been not quite a quarter and waxing, which meant it set about four hours after sunset this time of year.

"It was nothing then?" Stephen said.

"Well, it was unusual in that the man was crying — at times sobbing almost hysterically. He sounded so troubled that I started to get dressed. He needed comfort."

"And the woman? How was she dealing with this?"

"Not well, to my way of thinking. She kept saying, 'You must do it. Think of the child. They will tell even after this. Getting it back won't stay their tongues. If he finds out, he will kill it. It's the only way.' It was all very odd. Not comforting at all. Don't you agree?"

"What did the man say?"

"He said, 'I know.'"

"That's all you heard? 'I know'?"

"Well, there is one more thing. The woman said, 'Give it to me. You must. It cannot be found.' The man replied, 'I will not part with it.' He was very heated about it, anguished even."

"Anything more?"

"No." The priest put his hand on his door latch. "Except that the woman demanded again that she must have it. There was the sound of a scuffle for a moment. They spoke no more that I heard after that."

Chapter 19

When Stephen reached the end of the lane, where the town gaol sat across Peascod Street from the barbican, Rykelyng and his men were calling at the gate to open and let them in. Not wanting to be seen by them and having to face Rykelyng's wrath unnecessarily, Stephen hung back until they vanished inside. There was no use courting trouble if it could be avoided.

He wondered what Rykelyng would say to Prince Edward. Nothing favorable, of course. There was no doubt that Stephen was responsible for Ernulf's death and the loss of the horses. The truth was, his charge had been a reckless and foolish thing to do, a man had died because of his mistake, and the spies had got away. There was no getting around it.

Stephen leaned against the corner of the gaol, thinking about this for some time.

After a while, his thoughts drifted to the problem of Hafton. This pretend marriage hadn't solved the problem; it had only put off the reckoning. It either came to him or went to Ida. If he seized it, she would be cast out without means or property. Such a girl was unlikely to find a husband; no one wanted a poor gentry girl. He imagined her ending up like Mistress Bartelot, born of a gentry family, the last of many daughters, sent off to marry a merchant because no one would have her, and who had died leaving her penniless. Could he do that to Ida? He had promised Elysande, her mother, he would provide a good dowry, but the truth was, the manor hadn't much surplus to spare for it. This was the main reason he had not pressed his claim through the courts. He had dithered, hoping that the problem would solve itself. But of course, problems like this never did.

On the other hand, if he allowed the manor to fall to her, she became a king's ward again whom the king could marry off to anyone he chose.

"At least I am the part owner of an inn," he said to himself. "I can fall back on that and my garret room if all else fails and the money runs out."

These were unpleasant thoughts. He pushed them out of his mind by recalling what the old priest had told him. He tried to fit it with what he already knew about Father Giles and his death. People wanted the cross, not just the spies, but also this woman. It sounded like there had been a struggle. Giles could have been killed in that struggle, but the cross was around his neck when he was found. So, he wasn't killed over the cross at all, but for some other reason. Try as he might, he could not fathom what that reason might be. He wished Gilbert were here so they could talk it over.

Gilbert, though, was likely snug in his bed, his stomach gurgling from supper. That's where Stephen should be himself, in bed at least; supper was not a possibility at this hour. He pushed away from the wall and headed downslope toward Morstreet.

Clouds were closing in, blotting out the stars, deepening an already dark night. His breath came in frosty jets. And quiet: his boots scraping on the dirt and dislodging pebbles here and there seemed unnaturally loud. He heard someone moving on the parapet above and saw a man's head in a crenellation.

He came to Morstreet and turned down hill toward the river. The dark houses on either side, with the castle looming above to the right, reminded Stephen of canyons he had ridden down in Spain, although those were far more vast and impressive than any street in a little English country town. He experienced a pang of longing for Spain. He had been happy there with Rodrigo and his men. War had been a game, deadly to be sure, but a game he had felt he was winning, finding a good woman and building a fortune. But war was not a game, of course. That fact had come home when a Moor cut off his foot on the battlements of Rodrigo's castle. He and his wife Taresa had been fortunate to escape before the castle fell and the Moors killed every man inside.

The street flattened out and curved left toward the river.

The Corpse at Windsor Bridge

Stephen crossed the wooden bridge over the mill race and came to the Wily Minstrel Inn. It was dark and locked up tight, of course. It had to be midnight. No one was awake.

He was desperately tired and sore from his fall from the horse and the walk back. He wanted inside more than anything. His palm was poised to bang on the door when a glimmer of light impinged on the corner of his eye. The glimmer reflected off a wooden post by the bridge that boatmen used to tie off their vessels. Someone had a fire going on the wharf.

Which meant that someone was awake there in the middle of the night.

Why would someone be awake on the wharf at night?

Stephen's hand fell to his side, the inn's door unmolested and the innkeeper's sleep undisturbed at the moment.

His feet carried him limping to the path at the foot of the bridge and down to the wharf.

The source of the fire was readily apparent: a campfire was burning just outside a shed. A small figure was sitting before the fire. He remembered seeing the shed before, and children within it.

Stephen approached the fire and the figure, resolving into a boy of about twelve, climbed to his feet.

"What you doing here, my lord?" the boy asked. The question was not politely made, the "my lord" rendered sarcastically.

"I'm not sure," Stephen said. "Mind if I share your fire?" He noticed that the boy had a large bell in his hand. He gripped it as if it was a weapon, although it wasn't large enough to damage anyone even if hit over the head.

"I don't know," the boy said. "That depends."

"On what?"

"On what you got in mind. We don't get many lords wandering down here this time of night who have good intentions in mind."

Stephen settled cross-legged by the fire. "I'm not a lord, as you can well see, and I've a mind only to ask a few questions."

The boy sat down too, but didn't relinquish his grip on his bell. "You might be a lord for all I know. You were one of those with the prince when they found that dead man."

"Yes, he asked me to find out why he died, and who did it."

"You think it was us?" He seemed amused at this.

"You don't look big enough to toss a grown man in the river." Stephen glanced in the shed. There were the forms of at least six children sleeping inside. "Unless you all got together."

"It weren't us. You can bet on that."

"It's a bet I'm not willing to take."

Not far from where Stephen sat, there was a pile of white feathers and a swan's head and feet. The boy noticed Stephen's glance and looked alarmed. The swans along the river belonged to the crown. It was a poaching offense to kill one. The softest penalty was the loss of a hand.

"You should get rid of that," Stephen said.

The boy got up and collected the remains of the swan. He threw them in the river and then came back to the fire.

"You going to say anything?" the boy asked.

"No," Stephen said. He plucked two feathers that clung to the boy's coat and put them in the fire, where they flared and curled up. "I don't care about a dead swan. What's your name?"

"People call me Alf."

"Do you live in the shed, Alf?"

"I do."

"It doesn't look too comfortable."

"It keeps the rain off. I've slept in worse."

Stephen smiled. "So have I."

He waved toward the fire. "Can't sleep?"

"Nah," Alf said. "I'm working."

"Working?"

"That's right. I ain't no vagrant. I'm a working man. We're all working men. Or working girls."

"What do you work at?"

"I'm a watchman, I am," Alf said with pride.

"Of what?"

"Of the wharf! What else would I be watching from here? We get paid to keep an eye on the boats." Alf toward the boats tied up not far away.

"So, one of you is awake every night, all night?"

"For a rich lord, you're really quick."

"Thanks. I take pride in merely being a little stupid. There wouldn't happen to be any of that swan left, would there? I missed supper."

"Nah, all gone."

"I thought that might be the case." Stephen glanced over his shoulder at the bridge. "One of you would have been awake when that fellow went into the water."

Alf stirred the coals with a stick. He added a splint of wood. "That was me. I've got the midnight watch."

"What did you see?"

"A fellow came down from the ferry. It sticks in my mind because he was carrying a stolen anchor. Those things are heavy. He could barely get along with it."

"Did you see his face?"

"No."

"Was this a big man?" Stephen asked.

"No, he was rather short, much shorter than you are, that's for sure. And I thought he walked funny, although that might have been the anchor dragging on him."

"You didn't raise the alarm at this theft?"

"I didn't know for sure it was theft. Anyway, I'm not paid to protect the ferry. What happens there is their lookout."

"How do you know the anchor was stolen?"

"Because I heard people complaining about it and the loss of the rope the next day. Ropes and anchors aren't cheap for ordinary folk. Not like you'd know that, though."

"I know about rope, but I've never had the occasion to price an anchor."

"Well, take my word for it."

"I will. What happened when you saw him?" Stephen asked.

Alf shrugged. "He walked on by. The fire had died and I'd not fed it yet. He never looked in my direction, and I doubt he even knew I was there. At least he gave no indication."

"That's all?"

"Well, just a short time later, there was two men yelling at each other on the bridge."

"What did they say?"

"Damned if I know. They talked French. I don't have no French. I'm an Englishman." He frowned. "But it sounded like an argument, though. Loud and angry. If I had to guess, it sounded like one of them was making a demand and the other was refusing."

"That was all?" Stephen asked.

"It went on until they came to blows."

"You saw them fight?"

"It was too dark for that," Alf said. "The moon was well down, and it was overcast, like tonight." Alf pointed to the bridge. "You tell me if you can see the bridge and people on it!"

"How do you know they were fighting?"

"From the grunting and the pounding they were giving each other."

"How did the fight end up? Could you tell who won it?"

"No. I heard heavy breathing, some thumping about. There was a bit of motion, something moving in the dark, you know what I mean?"

Stephen nodded.

"Then there was a splash," Alf said. He threw up his hands. "That was it. That's all I seen."

The Corpse at Windsor Bridge

Stephen awoke in the shed with a stiff neck from the lack of a rest for his head. He sat up and rubbed his face, his beard rough and prickly under his hands. The fire was out and only one of the child watchmen was awake.

Although the sun was up enough to provide some light, a fog so dense that Stephen could not see the opposite riverbank gave the world a closed, compressed feeling and the air a metallic smell. Two shadowy figures could be seen moving about the boats on the wharf. The little watchman glanced at them, unconcerned; they must be boatmen coming to work.

Stephen rose and kicked ash over the remaining coals so that some might remain alive and the fire rekindled in the evening without trouble.

When he turned around, Alf was sitting up.

Stephen indicated the boats. "Which one of them has an anchor like the one you mentioned last night?"

Alf glanced over the boats with a professional air. He pointed to one anchor, a stone circle with a hole in the middle for the anchor line. "That one."

Stephen squatted and picked up the anchor. It was heavy, all right, but he thought he could carry it some distance without too much trouble.

A boatman a couple of boats down saw what he was doing. "Hey!" he called.

"He's all right, Herman," Alf said.

"What's he up to?" Herman asked suspiciously.

"Nothing illegal," Alf said. "Just taking his morning exercise."

"That don't belong to him!" Herman replied.

Stephen put the anchor down. "Sorry. Lifting anchors helps crack my back. It gets stiff from sleeping on the ground."

"What you doing sleeping on the ground out here?" Herman asked, for he had seen Stephen come from the watchmen's shed.

"Argument with the wife," Stephen said. "She kicked me out last night."

"You?!" Herman said, disbelieving since he had to look up to make eye contact as Stephen was much taller than him.

"She's a terror when she gets going," Stephen said.

He dug into his purse for a penny, which he gave to Alf. "Thanks for your help. Get some fresh bread for yourself and the others. Don't gamble it away."

Alf smiled as he closed his fingers about the penny. "I don't know what good I did you, but you are welcome just the same."

Stephen took a few steps, then turned back.

"I was wrong," he said to Alf. "There's more you can do for me, if you're willing."

Alf looked at the penny on his palm. "Like what?"

"Can you swim?"

Chapter 20

Herman maneuvered his boat through thick fog to the spot where Stephen reckoned Giles' body had been found. He remembered the place because it had been near a piling streaked with bird shit more than the others, but the fog, which at times even obscured the banks on either side of the boat, made finding it difficult.

Herman steered the boat along the pilings until Stephen called out for him to stop. He thought this was it. The supports under the bridge and over that particular one were choked with old bird nests.

"Here," Stephen said. "I think we're above it."

Herman turned the bow of the boat against the current and rowed easily to keep it in place.

"Over you go," Stephen said to Alf.

Alf, stripped naked since he had no braises, threw off his cloak and shivered. He did not look enthusiastic. He tugged at the rope tied about his waist as a safety line and took up another length of rope.

"How deep is it here, do you think?" Stephen asked as Alf put a foot on the saxboard.

"Probably your height and half again," Alf said.

He took a great gulp of air and stepped into the black river.

Alf resurfaced sometime later and clung to the side of the boat to recover his breath.

Then he dived again.

It took three more dives before Alf gasped, "I've got it! Haul away!"

"You first," Stephen said. He held out a hand and pulled Alf into the boat, then turned to the other rope.

He hauled away. The rope was slack for a moment, then progress halted with a jar. There indeed was something heavy on the other end.

Stephen reeled in the rope with great tugs of his arms, hand over hand, getting pretty wet, until the thing became visible in the dark water: a round stone anchor like the one he had lifted on the wharf.

Another length of rope had been tied through the hole, and it had been cut cleanly after two feet or so.

Stephen drew the anchor into the boat. It landed with a thud against the thwarts.

"Careful, there," Herman said. "You might knock a hole in her and we'll all go swimming then."

"And I'd owe you for a boat," Stephen said.

"Come to think of it, I wouldn't mind getting a new one, sir."

"Some other day, perhaps," Stephen grinned. "Let's get to shore."

Stephen lugged the anchor to dry land when the boat reached the wharf, getting soaked to the knees as he clambered up the bank.

Gilbert and Ida were waiting there.

"What have you been up to?" Ida asked. "I was so worried when you didn't come back last night. Then we heard your voice from the window. Where have you been? Have you been out on the river?"

"Look what I found," Stephen said.

"I see it," Ida said. "Why are you carrying an anchor?"

"It's what held Father Giles down so that he died."

"Oh?" Ida seemed less interested in the anchor than in Stephen's disheveled state. "Come on, we need to get you cleaned up. You are a mess."

Herman, meanwhile having secured his boat, stared openmouthed at Ida. The top of her head came barely to Stephen's shoulder and her face, visible in the deep hood of her voluminous cloak, was sweet like that of an angel.

"This is the wife who kicked you out?" Herman burst out.

"You said I kicked you out?" Ida asked Stephen ruefully.

"I, er, well, yes," Stephen said. To the others, he added, "She is more than she appears."

Ida smiled at Herman. "He has a tendency to misbehave. I am working on that."

"I wish you success, my lady," Herman said. "I've not had much to do with your husband, but he does seem to have a capacity for mischief. Begging yer pardon, sir."

"That is truer than you know," Ida said.

Cleaning up had to wait, however.

Alf fetched the owner of the stolen anchor from the ferry, a transplanted Dutchman named Henrik.

Henrik identified the recovered anchor as the one taken three weeks ago, from a mark carved into one side, Y.

"Getting it back has to be worth something to you," Stephen said as Henrik bent to fetch it away. "That water's cold and dark. It was not an easy thing."

Henrik hesitated because Stephen was right.

"Three pence should do it, don't you think?" Stephen asked.

"Three pence!" Henrik howled as if he had been wounded. "It cost me five new!"

"Come on, Henrik," Herman said. "You know you can't get a decent anchor for less than eight. Give the boy three. Otherwise, he gets to keep it."

"But it's mine!"

"You lost it because you can't take care of your goods. The boy found it, at great cost to himself. Look — his lips are still blue! Finders are keepers. And you should make that four. You owe me one for taking him out there."

Henrik fumed but gave in. "All right. But what I don't get is how you knew it would be there."

Alf pointed a thumb at Stephen. "It was his lordship's idea."

Henrik shot an inquiring look at Stephen, who shrugged.

"Just a guess," Stephen said.

Seeing that this was all the explanation he would get, Henrik handed over the money and left with his anchor in the direction of the ferry.

Herman put Alf's share in his hand.

Alf regarded it with disappointment. "I'd have sold the thing for more."

"We have to keep the peace on the river, boy," Herman said. "It don't do to have rivermen angry with each other. What if you're out there one day and get in trouble and Henrik's the only one around? Do you want him to just sit by and have his revenge?"

Chapter 21

Stephen, Ida and Gilbert climbed the hill amid a stream of carts and people on foot headed to the Saturday market, which seemed to have got going late because of the fog.

Stephen left them at the pillory in the market so that Ida could wander about seeing what was for sale, and generally amusing herself, with Gilbert for companionship. His initial worries about the possibility of trouble with the FirzAllan men had subsided a bit. As long as they stayed in the market surrounded by people and didn't wander into some alley, they should be safe.

His objective was to question Isabel Gascelyn further. He crossed to the barbican and announced his name to the gate warden. He walked on after he did so and was surprised when the warden hurried to get in front of him.

"You're not to be allowed in, sir," the warden said.

"What do you mean?" Stephen asked, dumbfounded.

"Orders," the warden said.

"I've been given safe passage."

"I know that was so, but it's been rescinded."

"By whom?"

"Somebody. I don't know. I just follow orders."

Stephen was of a mind to demand to speak to the officer of the watch, but before he could open his mouth to do so, there were shouts in the bailey and a stream of spear-carrying sergeants marched through the gate toward him.

The gate warden said, "You'll have to move away, sir. They'll take no excuse and knock you over, no matter who you are."

As Stephen retreated toward the market, the sergeants burst out with cries of "Make way! Make way!"

The people in the market had no idea yet why they had to make way, but since people were used to being shoved aside for the noble born, they yielded as far as they could, which caused a press of bodies about some of the market stalls, whose frames wobbled dangerously. Stephen struggled through to Ida at the edge of the crowd, but Gilbert disappeared in the confusion. Stephen kept an arm around Ida as they were among those thrust back against the frame of a stall and nearly fell over.

A procession of mounted men trotted their horses through the barbican and turned left toward the fields east of the castle. At its head was Prince Edward.

Edward's eye caught Stephen's and then swept on as if he was not there at all.

FitzAllan, at the prince's elbow, spotted Stephen and Ida as well. His face contorted with a gloating sneer, and he pointed directly at Stephen and laughed before he rode on.

"I don't like the look of that," Ida said. "That foul man is up to something."

"I suppose we'll find out what it is soon enough," Stephen said.

Ida shivered. "Soon enough to duck out of the way, I hope."

Rykelyng, who was in the party, saw them, too. Rather than ride on, he broke out of line. He motioned for the sergeants to break their cordon for him, and rode up to Stephen.

"The prince bids me to tell you that your services are no longer needed," Rykelyng said, his lips curled with hatred. "It seems you are not up to the task he set for you."

"I am sorry about your brother, you know," Stephen said.

"I'll have satisfaction for him," Rykelyng said. "You can be sure of that."

He reined about, used his whip on the heads of some market goers who were in the way, and cantered to catch the tail of the procession.

When the prince's party had gone by, the armed sergeants withdrew into the castle and the market returned to its normal bustle.

"So, that's why you're out here instead of in there," Ida said.

"Yes. I am not wanted now."

"Are you reconciled with that?"

Stephen wrinkled his nose. He should say that he didn't care. But he did. "It is what it is."

"I see," Ida said, eying Stephen with an expression that said she did not take his attempt at unconcern at face value. "Well, whatever your feelings truly are, there is nothing to keep us here any longer."

"It seems so," Stephen replied. "But first, there is the market. It seems like a fine one. And the day is turning sunny and warm. Shall we take a look at what's on offer? Or do you want to rush off?"

"You — interested in the market?" Ida asked.

"I've no interest in markets. I'll just take my turn keeping you out of trouble, since Gilbert seems to have disappeared."

"You're not the sort to keep anyone out of trouble," she said.

They turned to find Gilbert extracting himself from a pile of those who had fallen over during the press. Ida held out a hand to help Gilbert to his feet. He brushed the dust from his coat, which included a footprint on the middle of his chest, muttering about being treated like a doormat.

"A rather plush doormat," Stephen said.

"You wouldn't like it if it had been you," Gilbert grumbled. "The fellow didn't even say he was sorry. What is the matter with the world! Rudeness and self-indulgence everywhere you turn these days."

The market was indeed a magnificent one. There were the usual rolls of brightly colored linen and wool; pots and kettles of iron and some in bright red copper, with ladles and spoons and prongs, and griddles, grills, pans with legs on them and without, trivets, and spits and stands for roasting meat; arrays of colored tiles for decorating a house; boxes and chests, some elaborately carved, some with tooled metal at the corners and at the locks; a table full of ropes of various lengths and sizes; another table strewn with all sorts of knives and cleavers; a lot of pottery, and one table with something quite new that attracted a crowd: glass goblets of red, blue, green and yellow; people selling surplus grain out of the backs of carts; one cart loaded three times the height of man with fresh hay, with a boy perched on top of it; racks of leathers; a shoemaker's transplanted shop where he worked behind the counter making a turn shoe for a woman sitting on a stool; and more, much more.

Stephen was contemplating buying honeyed buns for the three of them from a passing vendor, her wares set out on a board that hung by straps from her shoulders, when Ida tugged his elbow and pointed between two stalls on the north edge of the market.

"I wonder where she's going," Ida said.

"Who?" Stephen asked, his attention on the buns which were getting away, taking their mouth-watering aroma of sweetness and yeast with them.

"Princess Leonor. She's just come out and gone toward the bridge."

The appearance of a princess taking a stroll in public was sufficiently unusual to provoke comment. Indeed, others about them were pointing and remarking about it.

Stephen edged over to get a better look. A small procession of women was gliding down Morstreet beneath the western walls of the castle. He could only see their backs now, so there was no telling for certain that the princess was among them. It was a matter of only passing interest, anyway. Or would have been if one of the women hadn't paused to get a stone out of her shoe. Stephen saw her face as she stooped and half turned.

It was Lady Isabel.

Prudence and good judgment told him that he should turn away and let the matter lie. But his feet had a different opinion. Without thinking about it, he stepped through the stalls, passed by the pillory where a baker was doing punishment for short-weighting his bread, and followed the women down the hill.

"What are you doing?" Ida hissed as she reached his side. She tugged his arm, guessing what was in his mind. "Let it go."

"I won't be but a moment," Stephen said. "I just need a word with her."

"With whom? The princess?" Ida was incredulous.

"No, Lady Isabel."

"Lady Isabel? What do you mean to do?"

"I have … questions. Just a few questions."

Ida clutched Stephen's arm to hold him back. "Gilbert! Help me! Stop him!"

"I'm afraid there is nothing we can do, my lady," Gilbert stammered, wringing his hands. "He is a force of nature. We can no more contain the wind."

Quailing at her furious scowl, he hastily added, "I think Lady Ida is right. Let things lie as they are. You recall Father Bernard's warning! Why would you delve into matters where lives are in the balance when you don't have to? Surely, you must realize that one of them might be yours. Perhaps there are secrets involved that should not be known."

Stephen had no answer to this. They were right. But he removed Ida's hand from his arm, and started after the women anyway.

The women were well down the hill by this time and turning the corner around the castle's northwest tower. He wondered where they were going as he hurried after them. There wasn't anything he could think of in the lower town that might interest the princess: a few taverns and inns, the smelly tanneries and the slaughterhouse. Going to feed the swans, perhaps? A boat ride on the river?

As he rounded the northwest tower, the women were filing through the gate of the little chapel where the road bent toward the river.

Several women stood about the doorway to the chapel, and eyed Stephen with suspicion as he pushed through the gate. Neither the princess nor Isabel was among them. Had they gone inside? He could not think of a reason why they would do so. If they wanted to pray in a chapel there were two perfectly good ones in the castle. They didn't need to walk here.

Stephen started to go around the chapel to the little graveyard behind it. One of the ladies-in-waiting saw his intention and said sharply, "You will remain here!"

Stephen kept going without responding.

Princess Leonor and Lady Isabel were in the graveyard by Giles' grave, a bare oblong mound.

The women pivoted toward him, surprise on their faces.

"What are you doing here?" Leonor demanded. She spoke in Castilian and her eyes went over Stephen's shoulder to see if any of her ladies had come after him.

"Searching for the truth," Stephen answered in Castilian as he came up to them. It occurred to him that the princess' choice of language, one probably not spoken by any other of her ladies than Isabel, meant she anticipated their conversation was one she did not want others to understand.

"Sir, the prince no longer has any need for your services," Leonor responded.

"Perhaps his grace no longer has an interest in knowing how or why Father Giles died. But do you want to know?" Stephen asked.

Leonor hesitated.

"I do," she said in a low voice. She glanced at the chapel, where three of her ladies-in-waiting were peering at them. She motioned them to be gone and they ducked out of sight. "Do you know?"

"I have no direct proof, but I think I know enough to put together what happened. But I need to ask Lady Isabel a few questions to be sure."

"Very well," Leonor said.

"Perhaps I should do so in private."

"She can say before me what she has to say," Leonor said. "We have no secrets from each other."

"As you wish, your grace," Stephen said.

He turned on Isabel. "That was you outside Saint John the Baptist's Church the night he disappeared, wasn't it?"

"I don't know what you're talking about," Isabel said.

"The priest of the church overheard you. Shall we have him identify your voice?"

"I should call your bluff."

"What is this about?" Leonor asked.

"Father Giles had a jeweled cross," Stephen said. "It was given to him by a lover. The spies at the Golden Swan stole it. He arranged to steal it back. That happened the night he disappeared. He met the thieves at the church where he paid them and recovered the cross. Isabel met him there."

"Did you, Isabel?" Leonor asked, bewildered.

Isabel's mouth tightened. "All right. I did."

"How did you know to find him there?" Stephen asked.

"He told me his plan to … to pray at the church in the town." Isabel did not go on.

"You know there was more to it than that," Stephen said. "He went there to get the cross back. The cross the gang of spies stole from him. A priceless object they kept to force him to spy for them."

Isabel did not acknowledge this. She said bitterly instead, "He was a charming man, and could be delightful. But he was utterly without guile or cunning. He could be brought to say whatever was in his mind. All it ever took was a little coaxing, a show of sympathy, a few bats of the eyes. A man like that is a dangerous fool."

"What is this?" Leonor cried.

"Giles was a despondent man after his affair with a noblewoman ended," Stephen said. "He drank heavily at the Golden Swan, and, somehow, he mentioned the affair to one of the whores who worked for the gang. The gang managed to steal the cross, probably when he had passed out in one of the upper chambers. They undoubtedly threatened to expose the affair, using the cross as evidence, if he refused to spy for them."

"Oh, dear God!" Leonor gasped.

"How did you and Winnefrith get out of the castle?" Stephen asked, turning his attention back to Isabel. "The sally port?"

Isabel smiled without humor. "Of course — that's how you stole your wife away from FitzAllan."

"Well, was it?"

"We went out just after dark."

"You and Winnefrith."

"Yes, me and Winnefrith."

"Why take him with you?"

"He insisted on going. He was just as concerned about Giles as I was."

"What concern was that?"

"We feared for his mental state. We feared what he might do. He told Winnefrith that he was tired and he wanted all his troubles to end."

"I don't think that's why you went."

"How dare you doubt my word!"

"I wouldn't doubt it if you told the truth, but I don't think you do. No, you went to the church to see if you could get the cross back from Giles."

"I should never have given it to him in the first place," Isabel said heatedly. "If my husband finds out, the consequences will be terrible."

"Is that why you urged Giles to kill himself?" Stephen asked.

"Giles killed himself?" Leonor cried, aghast.

"He tied himself to an anchor stone and threw himself off the Thames bridge," Stephen said.

Leonor's hands flew to her mouth and she turned her back.

"Well?" Stephen demanded of Isabel.

"Answer him, Isabel!" Leonor said.

"It was the only way," Isabel said. She shrugged. "It was his idea. Not mine, and he knew it was the right thing to do." She waved in the direction of the upper town. "The spies were blackmailing him. The fool tattled to a whore one night when he was drunk and feeling sorry for himself, as he says. She was in league with the spies, and they threatened to expose our secret if he didn't spy for them. They demanded to know what Edward and Leonor said in confession as well as in private conversations. He also foolishly made it known that he overheard Edward's councils from the balcony in the chapel. They stole the cross as proof of their accusations if they had to make them. Giles was in anguish about what to do. He could not violate the sanctity of the confessional. And he could not bear betraying his dearest friends. But the prospect of the secret getting out was even more terrible."

"So, you kept whispering in his ear that the gang would make its accusations even without the cross. Stealing it back availed him nothing," Stephen said.

"It was the truth! My husband would have taken the accusations seriously."

"Why, because you have cuckolded him before?"

Isabel ignored that accusation. "There would have been an investigation. Winnefrith would have been put to the test. Every man confesses under torture."

"Why Winnefrith?"

"Because he knew, of course, you idiot."

"And with Giles dead, there would be no point in the gang making accusations."

"You see so clearly when a place is set before you."

Stephen was about to go on, but he paused to look at Leonor, who was sobbing soundlessly.

"Winnefrith came with you not out of concern for Giles' well-being," Stephen said to Isabel, "but to help with your plot to push Giles into killing himself."

Isabel did not answer.

"Winnefrith fetched the anchor stone," Stephen went on. "I have a witness to this. That witness also said that Winnefrith made a last attempt to recover the cross. He failed."

"Winnefrith was a better fighting man than Giles ever hoped to be," Isabel said. "I cannot imagine how he failed."

"Perhaps he underestimated how much the cross meant to Giles," Stephen said.

"He *was* attached to it," Isabel said bitterly.

Stephen looked around to see if anyone was close enough to overhear what he was about to say.

"You didn't give him that cross," Stephen said quietly. Even as the words left his mouth, he wondered why he said them. He had heard enough. He didn't need to hear more. And yet he could not stop.

"I did!" Isabel cried.

"It was another, wasn't it?"

"Do not dare to speak another word!"

"The priest at the church overheard you saying that the life of the child was in danger," Stephen said. "What child was that?"

Isabel's chest heaved.

"It wasn't your child," Stephen said. "You're not pregnant."

"But I am," Leonor said. She turned around, wiping tears from her cheeks.

"Is it Giles' child, your grace?" Stephen asked gently.

"Leonor!" Isabel said. "Say no more! For your life!" She stepped between Stephen and Leonor.

"There is a chance, but I don't think so," Leonor said.

"How did it happen, your affair?" Stephen asked gently.

Leonor took two paces in one direction and two back, moving her hands about. "I was thirteen. My parents and their advisors said I had to marry him. I always knew such a thing would happen, but somehow I thought it would not come so soon." She paced back and forth again. "I was not fully a woman then, and Edward wanted nothing to do with me after the first night." She shuddered. "It was painful, you see, having relations with him. Not pleasurable for him then, and certainly not for me. He sought comfort in the arms of a lover and eventually paid no attention to me. Me, I had nothing. Even the child he forced upon me a few years ago died.

"I was lonely. And sad. You have no idea what it is like to be sent away to a foreign country which you have no hope of escaping, forced to live among foreign people whose language and customs are odd and often repulsive, and with a husband who, until recently, wanted little to do with me." Leonor laughed humorlessly. "He didn't find me interesting until his lover died in the autumn. A fever, I heard. So many die of fevers in this country. Why is that?"

She went on, "Giles comforted me. We talked. He was kind and sweet. He spoke French so well. His voice was like music. I was weak. I gave into him one evening after confession."

"You gave him the cross."

Leonor nodded. "It was a foolish thing to do." She glanced at Isabel. "I regretted it as soon as I did so." She threw up her hands. "When I broke it off later, I demanded he return it. But he refused. His heart was broken and he was never the same afterward. He drank, he moped about, he followed me like a puppy. He said it was a remembrance of me. If he could not have my heart, he would settle for that." She reached into her collar and drew out the cross. "It was a gift from my mother. If Edward found it in Giles' possession, the secret would have come out. There is no telling what Edward would do, to me, or to the child."

"And you played on Giles' concern for the child by claiming it was his," Stephen said to Isabel. "He had to die so there was a chance the child would live."

She remained motionless, but a tightening of her lips was as good as a confession.

"It was necessary," Isabel said at last.

"I suppose it was after all," Leonor said. "But such a waste. Such a tragic waste." She looked balefully at Isabel but said nothing more.

There was silence in the graveyard for some moments.

Leonor looked down at the freshly turned earth. "He doesn't deserve to lie here, if what you say is true. Suicides have no right to burial in consecrated ground."

She turned back to Stephen. "What will you do with this knowledge?"

"Nothing," Stephen said.

"But what will you say to Edward if you are pressed?"

"If he ever asks, I would say the trail is cold. But it is most likely the spies killed Giles when he refused to steal your secrets for them."

"Even if you have to swear by God?" Leonor asked.

"If it saves an innocent life, then I think God will eventually forgive me."

"You are a peculiar man, Sir Stephen. To risk your soul for a stranger." Leonor drew in a deep breath and let it out. "Is there anything I can do for you?"

"I think not. By your leave, your grace."

Stephen bowed and left the yard.

Chapter 22

They left Windsor the next day, which was Sunday, and took the southern route home through Reading, Swindon, Cirencester and Gloucester to avoid lands held by Montfort adherents. Being low on ready cash, they could not afford a horse for Ida, so she rode the mare while Stephen walked.

It took six days to make the one-hundred-forty miles and Stephen had to walk the last twenty miles barefoot, as his boots gave out.

When they emerged from the forest at Ludford manor and Stephen glimpsed Ludlow from the high ground across the Teme, he almost broke down and cried with relief that they were nearly home.

Ida stopped the mare in the middle of the bridge and looked back at Stephen, who was limping along more slowly than he had been. She dismounted and waited for him.

"Let me see your feet," she said, bending down. "Good God, what a mess!" she added as she lifted one as a farrier might a horse's hoof. Ida set the foot down. "At least you're not bleeding. Get on the horse."

"I'll be all right," Stephen said. "It's not far now."

"I said, get on the horse, you fool."

"But how will it look? Me riding, and you walking."

"I don't care how it will look. I've had enough of your stubbornness! You'll ride from here out."

She scowled at him with her hands on her hips.

"You have a lot to learn about married life," Gilbert said, looking back, forgetting that Stephen had been married before. "You can't fight a woman when she is in that sort of mood."

Grumbling, Stephen mounted the horse.

Through Broad Gate and up the hill to Bell Lane they plodded, and a more welcome sight there never was as they turned in, Stephen's house in view across from the Broken Shield Inn.

Stephen grimaced with pain as his feet hit the ground when he slid off the horse. He stretched and flexed his shoulders, which ached. Then he looked in the front window into Harry's shop where he could hear noises of industry. Joan, the pretty blonde housekeeper, was turning the crank on a hand lathe while Harry, who had once been a legless beggar and now found work as a legless woodcarver, applied a cutting tool to shape it.

"What do we have there?" Stephen asked.

Harry and Joan turned with a jolt.

"God's whiskers! One interruption after another!" Harry exclaimed. He said to Joan, "Keep turning! We're almost done!"

Joan did not comply, however. She leaped up and called into the hall for Stephen's little son Christopher and rushed out into the street. She stopped short at the sight of Ida.

"You're back!" Joan cried in surprise. Her eyes wandered from Stephen to Ida. "How did you manage it? Mistress Bartelot said you were to be forced into a foul marriage with some loathsome fellow!"

"It is a rather long and shocking story," Ida said. "Filled with danger, intrigue and death."

Joan tapped her foot and crossed her arms. "Why is life like that where our lord and master is concerned? Well, get you in. You'll want supper. I've a good bit of soup left from dinner over the fire and the bread's not stale yet."

Gilbert took the mare and led her through the gate to the inn's stable, while Stephen picked up Chris, who had just run out of the house.

They all trooped into the hall, including Harry who had given up work on his project and swung behind them on his great muscular arms. Stephen put Chris down and sank into the house's lone chair, which was reserved for his use, although there were fresh wine stains on one of the arms showing that people had sat in it in his absence. Ida brought up a stool and put his feet upon it, as she called for Joan to fetch a pot of lard from the pantry.

Ida was rubbing some of the lard on the soles of Stephen's feet when Felicitas Bartelot appeared at the top of the front stairs. Shock made the deep vertical lines on her mule-like face stand out even more than usual.

"Ida!" Mistress Bartelot cried as she hurried down the stairs as fast as her voluminous skirts allowed. "What are you doing here!?"

"I've come home," Ida said, smiling but not ceasing application of the lard with her thumbs.

"Ow!" Stephen said.

"Be quiet," Ida said. "And hold still."

"Stop that right now!" Mistress Bartelot said, pointing a gaunt finger at Stephen's feet, a muscle in one cheek twitching with undisguised revulsion at the sight of the stump with Ida's hands upon it. "A lady does not do such things!"

"Well, I am sure that wives do so now and then, even gentle ones," Ida said.

"What are you talking about?" Mistress Bartelot screeched.

"We had to declare ourselves married in order to get me out of FitzAllan's hands," Ida said.

"You've … married … him?" Mistress Bartelot's finger changed its aim from Stephen's stump to his head.

"It looks as though we might be," Ida said. "My freedom depends on people thinking it's true."

"It is most unsuitable!" Mistress Bartelot said. She put a hand to her temple and began to sway. She might have fallen if Joan had not taken one of her arms and steered her to a nearby bench.

Mistress Bartelot pressed her face into her hands. "You cannot be married to that man. It is so wrong!"

Joan stood back from Mistress Bartelot once it was clear she would not topple over. She crossed her arms again. "You're actually married?"

"We declared ourselves so," Stephen said. "In front of Prince Edward and other leading figures of the realm."

"Oh, my," Joan said, sinking beside Mistress Bartelot.

"There is more to this than meets the eye," Harry said, regarding Stephen and Ida suspiciously.

"We'll tell you all about it later," Stephen said.

"Well, before you do that, you might want to see this." Harry propelled himself to the table and pulled himself up on one of the benches beside it with remarkable agility for a man with no legs; the people of this house were used to this sort of thing but it always startled those who did not know Harry. He held out a roll of parchment to Stephen. "It came by messenger yesterday. We don't know what it says, but it has a fancy seal on it, so it has to be important."

Ida brought the parchment over to Stephen. His heart skipped several beats when he saw the seal. He was familiar with it from his legal apprenticeship. It was the Privy Seal of the crown.

He unrolled the parchment and read it.

Ida bent over his shoulder for a look. But Stephen had allowed the parchment to curl up again.

"What does it say?" Ida asked.

"You remember that Hafton is held directly of the crown," Stephen said quietly.

"Yes. Father mentioned it."

"Prince Edward, in the king's name, has taken possession of Hafton and dispossessed us. You and me, specifically, by name. It is not spelled out, but two guesses to whom he has given it to in our place."

Ida slumped onto the arm of Stephen's chair. She put a hand on Stephen's shoulder and laid her head against his, disregarding Mistress Bartelot's scandalized expression.

"FitzAllan's revenge," Ida said.

"I am afraid so," Stephen said.

Epilogue

A week after Stephen and Ida returned to Ludlow, another messenger bearing parchments arrived from Windsor.

He was a handsome young fellow dressed all in black from thigh-high boots to cloak and hat, and he stepped into the front hallway without knocking or asking a by-your-leave after Harry shouted over the counter at his question that, yes, indeed, this was Sir Stephen Attebrook's residence.

The messenger jumped back, however, when Harry swung to the doorway, looked up at him, and barked, "State your business, sir!"

"Are you sure you belong here?" the messenger stammered.

"I damned well do," Harry said. "This is my shop. I repeat, sir, what do you want?"

It took a moment or two for the messenger to recover, for the sight of Harry, especially when his temper was aroused, was disconcerting. He was a solid block of legless fury that came no higher than a man's hip, yet gave the impression of being much larger; perhaps it was the shoulders and arms, which were massively muscled.

"I have a letter for Sir Stephen," the messenger said.

"Do you require payment?" Harry asked, as it was the custom for the recipient of a letter to pay for its delivery.

"No, that is taken care of." The messenger unslung a wax-covered black leather tube from his shoulder, unfastened the lid and extracted a rolled-up parchment. "If you are a shopkeeper, which is hard to believe, what business have you with me? I come for Sir Stephen."

At this moment, Ida, having heard Harry acting like a guard dog, came out from the hall. Even though she was supposed to be safe from FitzAllan, Harry had declared he didn't believe it, and he was likely to attack anyone barging into the house uninvited.

"Letter for Stephen, my lady," Harry said.

"I'll take it, thank you," Ida said, anxious that Harry not tackle the messenger, who seemed harmless, and throw him to the ground.

The messenger handed over the parchment with relief at not having to surrender it to someone as obviously disreputable, disrespectful and ill-mannered as Harry. "Your servant, my lady."

"And I am yours, sir," Ida said.

The messenger left.

"You're just going to stand there?" Harry said. "You're not going to read it?" He sounded as worried as she felt.

"I shall read it, Harry, and you'll find out what's in it in due course. Now back to work. You are wasting the day."

"Poor Stephen, having to put up with the likes of you," Harry pouted at the denial of his request. "I had no idea when you came here that you'd turn out like this."

"Like what, Harry?"

"So bossy. You make Joan and Edith Wistwode seem mild."

"Why, Harry, I did not think you capable of flattery."

Ida withdrew into the hall, where she examined the letter with more care. It was sealed with an elaborate seal in blue wax, but she could not identify it.

She broke the seal with her dagger and spread the letter out on the table, weighing down the corners with spoons and cups. She bent over the letter, her palms on the table supporting her weight.

She straightened up and tapped a finger to her mouth.

"What is it?" Joan asked from the central hearth fire where she was tending a cauldron. "More bad news?"

"Could you run up to the castle and fetch Stephen, please? He needs to see this right away." Stephen was on castle guard again, the only source of their income for the foreseeable future.

"Of course," Joan said and dashed out of the house with the alacrity of someone reporting a fire.

Stephen and Joan rushed in some time later.

"Is there trouble?" Stephen asked. Joan had told him of the arrival of the letter, and Ida's urgent request that he come immediately, and to his mind the letter could only mean bad news. They had already fallen farther than any of the gentry cared to, but there was always more room at the bottom.

"Have you ever heard of a place called Halton?" Ida asked.

"It's two miles, two and half from here," Stephen answered, bewildered. "Why?"

Ida pointed to the letter.

Stephen read the letter silently, his expression changing from concentration to consternation and astonishment.

The letter said:

> From Her Grace, Princess Leonor, to the Honorable Sir Stephen Attebrook, Knight, Greetings. —
>
> It has come to our attention that you have been dispossessed of your manor due to unpleasant circumstances of which you are aware and which we need not go into. We understand that this may put your family in straights that you may not deserve. In view of the invaluable service which you performed in the attempt to determine and to punish the murderer of our late servant and friend Father Giles de Twet, God rest his soul, even if unsuccessful, we think it mete that said service should not go unrecognized. Consequently, we are eager that you should be enfeoffed of our manor at Halton, if that is agreeable to you, with the understanding that you hold it from us as your lady, and shall come and do homage and perform knight service for it.

Stephen straightened up and turned to Ida. He was too stunned to speak.

"You turned her down once at Windsor," Ida said. "What will you do now?"

Historical Note

Edward I's wife is known to history as Eleanor of Castile. She was born in 1241 at Burgos, the daughter of Ferdinand III of Castile and Joan, countess of Pontheiu, a French county centered around Abbeville between Normandy and Flanders. Her birth name was Leonor. English writers in the 13th century rendered her name as Alienor or Alianor, and eventually the name was recorded as Eleanor.

Although the marriage of Edward and Leonor was arranged for political reasons, history records that it apparently became a love match, or at least one in which there was mutual affection. Edward is one of the few English kings who is not known to have had any mistresses or bastards. Leonor bore him at least fourteen children. All but five daughters and a son died as infants. She died herself at the age of thirty-nine on 28 November 1290. Edward was sorely grieved.

But history is never the whole story, and happy marriages do not always start off that way, or remain happy all the time. Who knows what troubles Edward and Leonor may have had that escaped the chroniclers?

One of the couple's fourteen children was a daughter, Katherine, born sometime during the spring of 1264. She died in September 1264, and is buried at Westminster Abbey.

In addition to being very beautiful, Leonor had a reputation as a shrewd businesswoman and she actively acquired lands and estates in her own name. What little that shines out of the chronicles about her reveals an intelligent and capable woman.

The making of a marriage was done much differently in the 13th century than it is today. No one was required to officiate, although the Church was pushing for priests to do so. All that was required was for the two people involved to exchange declarations of the intention to marry. It was advisable for this exchange to take place before witnesses, so that if there was a falling out and one sought to escape the marriage by denying the exchange of vows, the other of the parties had evidence of them. But witnesses were not required.

Made in the USA
Coppell, TX
22 March 2021